TRAIL OF DARKNESS

TRAIL OF DARKNESS

RJ Seymour

TRAIL OF DARKNESS is a work of fiction. Names, places, and incidents either are a product of the author's imagination or are used fictitiously.

A Book Furnace Publications Book

Published by Book Furnace Publications

ISBN 978-1-943266-03-6

First Edition Hardcover: January 2017

Cover Images: © Sascha Burkard/Adobe Stock
© Hektor2/Adobe Stock

To Wind:
My Strength, My Love, My Inspiration

Chapter 1

It's always darkest before dawn. That's what Liz's mother always told her. She didn't understand the saying, but she usually didn't understand much when her mom started talking all philosophical. Dad shook his head whenever she would get into one of her soapbox speeches, something he said that she didn't understand either. She never caught mom standing on a soap box, nor would the plastic hold her since it would crumble even when Chester and his pudgy little hotdog body stood on it.

Street lamps, their light burning away the darkness of the early morning, passed like signal flares as the family's Prius drove down Main Street. Liz leaned her head against the window and looked out, the cold glass a welcome feeling against her skin, watching the last drops of the rain that had welcomed them this morning chase each other down streaky paths to the frame where they disappeared.

Christmas was only a week away. Why did they have to move again? For the third time since she turned nine they had packed up their stuff and without warning moved, and even her mother wasn't happy about it this time. They had been fighting for two nights before they stuffed all of their clothes into suitcases and pushed what they could into the trunk.

Stevie didn't mind. He was too young. Liz looked at her brother, eighteen months old with his head tilted to the side in his car seat and a pacifier in his mouth. He was a good baby. Didn't cry much, outside of when he was hungry or wet. He loved playing with blocks. Liz smiled as her hands wrapped around the small box in her sweatshirt pocket.

When they got to their new home, it would be a Christmas gift to him. Something that would make him smile, though she knew he wouldn't understand. He was too young, but she was old enough to understand at least the difference each new home made.

They hadn't moved during the first nine years of her life, or at least she couldn't remember moving. One week before her ninth birthday her father broke the news to them. His job was finished up, but something new had come up outside of Chicago, Illinois. Liz didn't know where that was, but her mother, after coming from her room with red, swollen eyes had shown her on the family computer. It was a big city near the middle of the country, days and days of travel away from their home in Los Angeles.

Mom denied she had been crying, but Liz knew better. She was older than her mom wanted to admit, always talking about how she was still her little angel. Now at twelve, and after living only one year in another big city called Baltimore, they were moving north, to a town called Portswell, New York.

At first, she had been angry when her dad broke the news yet again. Becky down the street had finally gotten permission to invite her over for a sleepover, but that hadn't happened. They were supposed to spend the day before Christmas Eve eating candy canes and watching One Direction on Netflix, but the time to move had stepped in to ruin her plans again.

"This will be the last time, I promise," her father said while they sat at the dinner table.

Cooked ham with rice and vegetables. It was one of Liz's favorite. Even Stevie ate most of his plate, though a lot of it made it to the floor where Chester enjoyed dinner as well. Since it was one of the few times they all sat down at the table together, she figured it was everyone's favorite.

"You said that last time, Robert," her mom answered without looking up from her computer, which she had begun to use even at the dinner table.

She carried the silver case with her everywhere now, and Liz enjoyed playing the games on it. Candy Crush was her favorite, though Mom limited her to only times when she was too busy cooking or on the phone.

"I promise. The men at work told me that this was the last. There is nowhere to go after this," Dad said before swallowing the remainder of his Molson beer.

Liz wrinkled her nose at the smell anytime her father drank at the table.

"There is always somewhere else to go. There will always be somewhere else to go," her mom said.

Stevie never complained. Only when their voices raised did he start to cry. Liz always giggled when she watched him drop a piece of ham down to Chester. Mom and Dad never said anything when he did it. She wasn't sure they paid enough attention anymore to know what he had done.

The street lights quickly faded as the car made a hard turn to the left and headed out of town. Stevie stirred in his seat, gave a long sigh, and with a soft touch on his cheek from his big sister and he was back to his dreams. Chester opened his eyes and beat his tail a few times until she scratched behind his ears, then he laid his head back down and began his soft snoring.

Liz couldn't sleep, when they first turned away from home she had closed her eyes, intent on sleeping to help the hours go by, but dreams only came a little at a time. There were butterflies in her stomach, and they wouldn't stop. Dad had promised a house all their own, not an apartment with neighbors who were too loud. Mom even talked about having a garden where they could plant beautiful flowers in the spring, and pumpkins in the fall. Chester would have an entire yard to run around in and she could teach Stevie to ride a bike when he got older.

It was a dream come true for Liz. A home they could call their own, and her dad insisted it was the last time. They would stay, for the good or bad they would not move. She believed in him. Her mom would whisper under her breath, but Liz knew her dad wouldn't disappoint her. Not this time, not so close to Christmas.

Off into the east, the dark sky was beginning to turn shades of red with streaks of shadowed clouds as the sun would soon rise. Liz fought back a yawn of her own as the hum of the Prius' engine purred along. White snow blanketed the ground beneath the trees that began to thicken along the road where piles of leaves stuck out like tiny graves.

She liked snow. It meant no school and lots of fun, especially around Christmas. She trusted that it was a good sign; she could feel it in her heart she would be happy.

Chapter 2

Detective Marc Stutton sat behind the wheel of his 2001 Malibu, waiting and watching from the darkened corner of the Central Market parking lot. His contacts in the Maryland State Police told him there was an orange Prius with Maryland plates that was going to make its way into Portswell sometime this evening, and at the command of his department, it was his job to keep an eye on it. Not many people drove electric hybrids through this part of the state, the weather being too rough for vehicles without the four-wheel drive to survive the six to eight months that threatened snow off the lakes. He didn't expect it would be hard to spot them. Traffic was light this time of year as vacationers stayed south, preferring the warmth of Florida more than the bitter cold of the Adirondacks, and this night, in particular, had been dull, to say the least. Eight vehicles in three hours, nine if you counted the deer that had scampered its way past the front of the store and up the hill behind it.

They knew the date and the location, but they hadn't known the time, so sitting here in the dark by himself was his new assignment for the evening. This family of four was traveling from the south, and wherever they went, trouble was always quick to follow. His captain had thrown the file folder on his desk two weeks ago, a manila envelope more than an inch thick and heavy enough to knock his Syracuse Orangemen coffee cup to the floor when it landed.

"This should keep you busy for a while, Detective," Captain Veron said, the last word hanging in the air, before turning back to his office.

Marc had angered more than his fair share of captains and lieutenants in his life, but he still couldn't figure out Veron. They had only crossed paths twice in the three years Marc had been at the department, and each of those had been nothing but cordial and filled with sentences of very few words. Usually of the "OK" and "yes, sir" kind, and mostly from Marc's mouth. Working as a liaison from the Governor appointed Albany Person of Interest department, he had learned that his station and attitude always had to be mobile. This was his third assignment in less than ten years, never staying long enough to get the tenure he needed to actually put down some roots if he had been the kind of person to have any.

Flipping through the photographs with the thumb of his left hand, Marc could see the look on each person's face, how they stood, and how they walked in his mind without even the slightest glance at the faded photos. For two weeks he poured into the hundreds of documents, evidence collected and stored over the last fifteen years, from one side of the country to the other. Now the family was coming to his neck of the woods, both figuratively and literally, and their problem was his problem.

There were four of them, father, mother, daughter and youngest son. How much the kids knew would always be in question. The youngest, hardly a toddler, was of no concern, but the oldest was almost a teenager. They'd probably keep her in the dark as well, tell her stories that seemed reasonable and help cushion the constant moving and secrets. Marc pitied the younger ones for that. He had been an army brat before joining the state police. Fourteen states and three countries he had called home while growing up. Now in his forties, he couldn't stay in one place more than a few years. Sometimes he wondered if it was bad luck or if he was just born with a set of legs that wouldn't let him sit still.

It didn't matter, all that ever mattered was getting the job done. His father had taught him that, and it would probably explain why neither of them was any good with keeping women around. Over twenty years on the force, Marc knew what had been beaten into his persona was what allowed him to close over four dozen cases a year, the success that brought him both fortune and a lot of enemies both with a badge and without. Some cases were easy. Stay around the scenes long enough, and the perps were almost always dumb enough to return. You get a nose for these kinds of things the more bodies and bullet holes you count year after year. Then there are the ones that stick with you, deep down in the recesses of your mind they don't let you go.

He had been lucky, if he could call it that, up until two years ago. The change in assignment to the central Adirondacks had meant one thing for him, boredom. There were no more bullets to dodge or chasing perps through city streets and down darkened alleys. Drugs weren't traded on town corners like Pokemon cards shifting hands at the local elementary school. Here, in the middle of the endless forest, bears and drunken fights over the local high school football game was as eventful as it ever got. That was until little Tiffany Ambers.

Marc could see the white corner edge of her photo that stuck out from behind his car's visor. Wrinkled and sun faded, her face was never far from his mind, straight blond hair with eyes as blue as the sky. Her mother used to tell people how her smile could light up a room, and she had one hell of a voice. That little girl liked to sing and put on a show. He must have watched her performance at the town Christmas play over a hundred times. No one expected it would be one of the last times anyone saw little Tiffany alive. No matter how clean the light burned the paper, she would be waiting for him in the shadows. The case that he never closed.

Seven years old. Vanished from her parents' house on Christmas Eve without a trace. Two weeks later they found her night dress and teddy bear two miles into the park, torn apart by animals, or worse. The blood had been dry a long time, but the amount that had soaked into the cloth had sickened even the hardest of officers. The coroner couldn't give even a remote guess on the cause of death, and since they never recovered a body, the amount of blood present was all they had to go on.

Marc had been relentless, conducting his investigation while the parents were still mourning the loss of their child. Two weeks forced vacation were in order after the parents placed a restraining order on him. A little girl had vanished on his watch, and the only thing they had to show for it was blood soaked clothes and a teddy bear with a slit through its stomach.

How had she been taken?

There were no footprints or tire tracks leading to the house. All forensic evidence corroborated the parents' story that they had never left the house, and cadaver dogs never found even a trace of evidence that something had happened to her while she was at home. But something had happened in that two-story Victorian house, and before he ever let himself retire, he knew he'd find out.

Every Christmas since then had been a grueling nightmare for him. He would sit by the radio and wait for a call, just anticipating there would be another. These guys never stopped at one. If they got away with it the first time, they would do it again. He knew how they worked. For twenty years he had been wrapping his mind, delving deep into the darkness that fed them, and one day he would solve the mystery. How they ticked and what drove them over the edge. No one in the department or on the force would work as hard as he did. Not for Tiffany, and not for any other child out there. He was all they had, and he wouldn't let them down.

In the east, Marc could see the first signs of the coming morning burning away at the night and giving way to the gold rays of the sun as the sky stained itself red. Today was his day off. If the family didn't arrive before breakfast, he would grab something to eat when the market opened and head home. A call would have to be made down to Maryland. Once again their intelligence had proven less than reliable.

Fatigue burned at the corner of his eyes as he stretched his arms and then took a sip of his coffee, cold and stale as it had been for the last couple of hours. Running his hands over the open folder laying on the passenger seat, he could feel the edges of pictures as they passed over his fingertips. Eyes, piercing and dark, stared back at him. The mother and father with two young children hugging them, an appearance of normalcy that he knew was only a ruse. Grabbing his notepad, leather bound and nearing the end of its available paper, he opened where his pen held his spot and kicked on his cell phone for a little more light.

December 19th, AM. Arriving in unmarked Prius. Follow with caution.

So he knew he was here on the correct day. Lawrence damn well wouldn't be getting a Christmas card this year; if he just spent an entire night sitting in his car waiting for nothing, the man would owe him more than an apology. Only two more hours and he'd be heading home. Tossing his notebook back on the chair, Marc leaned back and let out a yawn he knew he'd been holding back for too long. These stakeouts were beginning to wear him thin. He was too old for this, and too grumpy after a night with no rest.

The sound of puddles splashing brought his eyes back to the road, the first distinct sound since as long as he could remember. It was probably the store opener or the morning newspaper man coming around the corner. Marc tucked his phone back into his pocket as he waited for the vehicle to come into view. If he were lucky, it would be the opener, and maybe he could talk them into getting the grill started early. Any excuse to get him out of the car for a cup of fresh, warm coffee.

With another splash, the Prius rounded the edge of Oxbow Lake and moved its way down Main Street. Its bright lights flashed across Marc's hood before continuing down the road, slow and steady as it passed through town. Marc could feel his heart jump-start as they had finally arrived. Reaching for his keys, he turned on the ignition and the trusty engine fired up without hesitation. Headlights on, he pulled up to the road just as the Prius slowed to ease around the left that followed the lake's bend as the highway headed back out of town. Breakfast and sleep now forgotten, Marc pulled away from the Central Market and followed the orange car at a safe distance, noting that he could see at least three heads in the windows and a car seat that had to be the youngest. He was in no rush; he wasn't there to stop them.

Follow with caution.

The words rang in his head, advice he had never followed when he was younger, but he was older now, and with age, he had learned how to follow orders.

Chapter 3

"It's beautiful isn't it?" Dad asked with Stevie lifted high on his right shoulder.

Cold air whistled by with leaves rolling like tumbleweeds as they stood in front of their new home. Liz didn't know what to think. Her mind was a mix of excitement and confusion as she leaned against the car. The house looked old, its white siding chipped and broken in several areas. Pale blue shutters were closed over the windows on the first and second levels and a blue porch with a railing that was broken in a couple places wrapped around from the front door to the back.

"You didn't say it would be a fixer-upper," Mom said before she kicked at the snow and gravel mix at her feet, her jacket bulging at the pockets where her hands balled into fists.

"They didn't say anything about it needing work, but we can do it," her dad replied. "Plus, this is all ours. No one is going to take it away."

Stevie squealed as her father tossed him up into the air. Chester barked from the car windows where he raced from the back seat to the front, his tail wagging a thousand miles an hour. He wanted to come out and play. Liz bet there were smells all over the place that he hadn't experienced yet, and several trees she knew he'd pee on immediately.

"It's going to be so much work, though," Mom sighed.

"That is what will make it ours, Amy. Stop being so down in front of the kids, we finally have a home."

Liz tapped on the hood of the Prius, Chester's barks bellowing out as he put his paws on the dashboard and wet nose against the windshield.

"Yes, Liz?" Her mom turned toward her while rolling her eyes.

"Can we go inside now?" Liz asked, more anxious to see her new room than she was to get out of the cold.

"Of course. Get Chester out of the car first."

Liz felt the smile stretch the frigid skin of her face as she turned and pushed the buttons to unlock the door.

3-4-5

Chester yipped as he jumped from the front seat and bounded into the snow that rose up to his hotdog belly. The cold powder didn't stop him as he jumped from pile to pile. There were three circles of yellow in the white field before he bounded in front of Liz and barked as he zig-zagged between her feet.

"Time to see what's inside," her father announced.

Stevie pointed to the front door as they took the lead, Liz and her mom following quickly behind. No birds sang in the brisk morning air as the snow and stone of the driveway crackled under their feet. Trees surrounded all sides of the house. Cleared for a large yard in all directions, the driveway was the only way in and out. Liz wondered if she'd be able to make any friends other than with the animals that lived in the forest like she was Cinderella or something, but her dad told her she'd like the house no matter if they were out in the woods or not.

"I bet it looks better on the inside," her father said as he stepped on the porch.

Wood creaked under his weight as he stepped toward the door, Stevie in one arm and the keys in his other hand. Liz stood with her mom away from the porch as they waited, the sounds of the house adjusting to her father growing as Chester began to bark loudly.

"Now, which key was it again?"

Chester ran in circles, faster, and his barking took on a more frantic pace as her father continued to struggle.

"Quiet it down, Chester," her mom barked. "Do you need any help, Robert?"

Liz stepped away as the little dog refused to quit. His antics turned angry as he bit at the wet bottom of her favorite jeans.

"Come here boy," Liz begged. The dog jumped into her arms but continued to bark. "What's wrong? It's OK, boy."

The way he kicked with his tiny legs, Liz struggled to keep the dachshund in her arms. He was staring into the sky, his tail standing stiff as he growled and barked. Liz squeezed him tighter as the creaking of the house grew louder than even his frantic cries.

"What is he barking at?" her mom demanded as Liz had to shift the small dog in her arms.

"I'm not sure, I think something has him scared," Liz replied.

With a straight grin, her mom walked over and placed a grip on his head, not exactly what Liz felt was comforting, but it did the job.

"It's OK, Chester. I know it's scary," she whispered, but pulled her hand back as he snapped his teeth at her fingers.

Liz ignored the look on her mother's face as she followed the little dog's small brown eyes. They were not concentrated on her mom but locked in a solid stare up at the top of the house. Wood screamed in protest with a small breeze that carried through their big yard.

SNAP!

"Mom!" Liz yelled as she closed her eyes and pushed as hard as she could into her mother.

The soles of her sneakers slipped on ice buried under the snow as she tried to move them both. Within two steps her knee crashed into the ground, the cold stone sending pain through her leg as she tumbled and Chester jumped free. Her mother stumbled backward just enough to avoid the falling shutter that smashed inches from Liz's legs.

"Oh my god!" Her father yelled as he cleared the steps of the porch in a single bound. Stevie stood at the door, his wobbly legs bowing as he held onto the wall. "Are you two OK?"

"Liz, are you hurt?" her mother asked frantically, her arms brushing at the snow and leaves that clung to Liz's winter coat.

"I'm fine, Mom. I think I scraped my knee, though," Liz answered as she chewed on her lip. She could feel the sting as the damp jeans rubbed against her knee.

Tears burned at the edge of her eyes as she sat up and saw the broken shutter that had exploded when it hit the ground. Wood splinters of blue and dark, rotted wood were scattered in the snow and dirt of the driveway.

"You saved us both, Liz," her mom said.

Liz gathered her feet under herself as her father lifted her off the ground.

"It wasn't me. Chester was the one barking at the house. He was trying to tell us it was going to fall."

"I always told you, Amy, that keeping that dog around was a good thing," her father chuckled through the smile that had returned to his face.

Chester barked as he jumped up at Liz's pant leg again, his tail a blur and tongue hanging out.

"You are a good boy aren't you?" Liz asked as she scuffled the little dog's ears.

"What are we going to do about that?" Amy asked.

Her mom waved her arm around at the carnage of debris that was now scattered in front of the house.

"I'll clean it first thing in the morning. Now, let's get inside and see what else we can find," her father said. "We are going to love it here."

Liz felt the squeeze of her mom's hand as she wrapped her fingers around her shoulder, the fingers digging deeper than she wanted. Together they followed her dad through the door. Stale, musty air escaped into the open as they entered the house. It wasn't great, and Liz could feel the butterflies in her stomach doing a dance that made her just a little sick, but it was home. Her father had promised her it was.

Chapter 4

"Remember to brush your teeth!" Liz's mom yelled from down the stairs.

Steam sat heavy in the air as Liz wiped away the mist that clung to the bathroom mirror. The smell of unopened windows and dust had filled the house, and the carpets were in bad need of a vacuuming, but at least the bathroom had been easy to clean, and the water was hot. Beads of condensation dripped down the silver surface as she looked at her reflection. Twelve years old and she still had the freckles of a little girl. She had been fortunate enough to avoid the acne her best friend Brittany suffered from. Her mother attributed it to the lessons of scrubbing her skin red every night that she had been taught since she was six. "One doesn't know when a pimple could erupt and it's better to always be prepared," her mom was fond of saying.

Inside, the house had been larger than Liz expected. Three full bedrooms filled the upstairs. The second largest she had claimed for herself and all the books she carried with her. A kitchen with a full separate dining room, a living room so large Dad said he was going to have to buy the largest TV he could find to fill it, a basement filled with spider webs and creaky wooden stairs and an attic that no one had gone up to yet.

Liz wanted to explore all of it. This was going to be their home; shouldn't they know everything now that they were finally here?

"There will always be more time for exploring, my darling," her father assured her.

Water swirled in circles around the sink as Liz watched the foamy toothpaste bubble before it went down the drain. How was she going to sleep tonight? There could be ghosts or goblins in the house, maybe even old, faded paintings of husbands and boyfriends who had gone off to war and never returned or dusty old love letters tucked away in discarded chests waiting to be read and given back to wrinkly old ladies sitting in nursing homes who had forgotten about the notes they had written to the loves of their lives some eighty years ago.

Liz smiled to herself at the thought. It felt like more of a cheesy Nicholas Sparks movie that Brittany would watch a thousand times than something that would really happen, but so much remained in this house to see and the butterflies in her stomach would not settle.

Placing her hands on the damp towel wrapped around her body, she could feel the bubbles churning. Dinner had been a delivered pizza from the local shop called Old Country Pizza. Dad had said it was the best pizza he had ever tasted, while Mom took a few bites and pleasantly agreed. Liz couldn't stomach much of it. The taste was fine, and the extra twenty minutes it took to arrive because the delivery guy got lost didn't bother her. The excitement of everything was what filled her up, and wouldn't let her go hungry. The sun had gone down, and deep shadows filled the house, giving it a darker feeling. Voices in her head told her of the scary things that hid in the darkness of vacant houses, yet inside she wanted to see more. They had three working flashlights in the car, and she knew where they were. Fear or not, she was going to explore. Stevie didn't seem to notice that they were in a new home at all. Crying when the vacuum ran, and squealing like a piglet in mud as Dad carried him around the house, at his age anything and everything was home to him.

"You almost finished up there, Liz?" Her dad yelled from downstairs. "Your mother and I have something for you if you hurry up."

Liz's heart quickened at the thought of a surprise. It had to be a present. She loved getting presents and knowing that it was still a week away from Christmas meant this would be something extra to add to all the stuff she would already be getting. Whenever they moved, she would get double the number of gifts. It was probably a way for her parents to say "I'm sorry" for forcing her to leave her friends behind, but she knew it wasn't their fault. Dad's work moved him around, and they'd done it so much recently it almost felt normal. The extra toys and clothes did help, though she tried not to let it show.

"Be right down, Dad!"

Running a brush through her shoulder length brown hair one more time, she was happy it laid down flat. With just the first hint of curling, it would be OK to leave it like this for the night. The mirror had fogged up again, so she ran her hand towel across the surface one more time.

No pimples, though she could see the spots near her nose and left temple still had a few clogged pores. It would have to wait until the morning. Her surprise waited for her downstairs.

Turning the old knob on the bathroom door, the metal hinges creaked even at the first few inches as the cold air rushed in and pushed the humidity out.

"Darn it," Liz whispered to herself.

She was only able to open it wide enough for a few fingers to get through before the box of bathroom supplies she had moved previously blocked her. Black permanent marker had the words "bathroom" scribbled across the top, and the cardboard had been hastily folded back over to keep it shut.

Feeling the piece of cheese still stuck between two of her back teeth, Liz kneeled down to rummage through the supplies to find the floss. She would be digging at the food all night if she didn't get rid of it.

Cans of hairspray and shaving cream, packs of new toothbrushes and combs littered the inside. Frustration built in her blood just enough to help her feel the humidity in the room as she shoveled everything around. There had to be floss somewhere in here, Mom would never let them run out of any needed items.

She was a stickler for always keeping her appearance up, even when she was alone in a new house.

"You OK up there, honey?" Her mom asked.

"Yep, I'll be right down. Just give me one more minute."

Liz was losing her patience. She removed a quarter of the contents and spread them around the linoleum floor, dark brown spades repeating in squares all across the bathroom.

A small white square box. There had to be one somewhere around here. Digging with her fingers, she forced her hand down to the bottom where everything you were looking for always found a way to land.

"Ah, there you are," she said to herself as her fingers wrapped around the tiny plastic case.

Lifting the floss out, light found the bottom of the box as she pulled her hand away.

LOVE YOU ALWAYS

The words were written in red glitter across the top of the card. What was a card doing at the bottom of the packed bathroom supplies? Shoveling more of her dad's shaving cream and razors out of the way, Liz pulled on the paper until she was able to hold it in her hand.

The stock was a light pink with deep red lettering. Hearts and ribbons of glitter framed the outside. It must have been an old Valentine's Day card from her father. She couldn't remember the last time she saw them do anything special for the holidays, so this must be something that her mom had held onto. The idea of reading words that her father had written years ago made the already active butterflies in her stomach jump.

I am nothing if but a leaf on the wind until I am in your arms. When we are together the world is whole, and we are what we were meant to be.

That was how the cover of the Valentine read. It was cheesy, and it reminded her of something you could buy at the local gas station.

Dear Amy,
No matter where you go, no matter what tries to separate us, we will always find a way.
You will be mine,
Your secret in the night,
Tony

Liz threw the card onto the floor before she pushed herself away from the box, as if it was on fire. Who was Tony? Why was there a love letter from him to her mom? This had to be an old card. Maybe it was from before her parents were married? But why would she keep it?

"Do you need any help, baby?" her mother called, her voice now much closer than the bottom of the stairs.

Liz could hear the steps creak as her mother continued her way up.

"No, I'm fine! Coming out now!"

The beat of her heart thundered in her chest as she shoved the card back into the box. Cans of hairspray and brushes banged around as she cleaned up her mess. There had to be a good explanation. Maybe she never knew she had kept it and in the haste of packing, accidentally put it in the box. A thousand explanations ran across Liz's mind as she finished replacing the last of the supplies.

"Coming down!" she yelled out.

Whatever it was would have to wait. Her parents didn't fight much, but when they did it got loud and angry. She'd ask her mom about it in the morning when they were alone. Dad had said he was running to the hardware store to get some supplies, so she'd talk to her then. No reason to bring it up now, she'd think of what to say to her mom tonight in bed. Maybe it would come to her before she fell asleep.

Cold air sent a shiver down her spine, its icy fingers tickling her back as she opened the door and headed down the stairs.

Chapter 5

Metal pots clanging together broke the stillness of the morning as Liz rubbed the edges of her eyes with balled fists. Sleep begged from the depths of her mind as the solemn promises of dreams and comfort begged for her to return, though the sun shone brightly from behind the cotton curtains. When did she fall asleep? Questions and anxious butterflies had filled her for half the night after her parents had finally told her to go to bed. Darkness came quickly this time of year, so the sky outside had been black a long time before her head ever hit the pillow, and though she hadn't found her alarm clock, she knew it must have been hours before she fell asleep. Yawning, she knew she could have only been asleep for an hour or two.

Cold air filled the room with a chill, the embrace of winter temperatures too much for the morning light to burn away. Liz pulled the thick comforter that her mother had unpacked for her up to her chin as she shivered away, comfortable in the little cocoon of warmth she had curled up into on her bed. Voices talked in hushed tones as her parents worked downstairs and the smell of breakfast began chasing away the memories of yesterday. The house was large but empty, and words carried greater distances out here in the silence of nowhere.

Tucking herself deeper under the light blue blanket, Liz reached for the small picture alcove that sat only a foot over the head of the bed. Almost empty and full of dust, her fingers quickly found what she was reaching for as she pulled her arm back under the warmth of the blanket and out of the frosty air.

Heavier than it seemed, the snow globe naturally tumbled in her fingers as she covered herself and the new gift under the thick covers.

Very little light penetrated the thick cotton as Liz rolled on her side and placed the ornament on the mattress beside her. Running her fingertips along the edges, she could feel the smooth nameplate along the front and the coarse, hard aluminum that wrapped around the base. A single lever in the back flipped the small light within the glass on and off, and with a tap, the inside of the globe lit up the darkness that filled the small campsite of her bed.

It was a simple toy. She could see the small flakes of white littered across the field where a single house stood. Identical to their new home, the white house stood solitary in the field, its blue shutters and porch almost the only color in the world other than the painted trees that lined the outer edge of the glass. Yellow light illuminated the globe through the windows of the house, giving the small world within an alive feeling as Liz flicked the switch from on to off and back. She stared into her own bedroom's window as she waited to see shadows cross in front, the toy a representation of life in her hand as it was in the real world around them.

With a few turns of her wrist, the white flakes swirled in the water of the globe, the air and the world a frenzy of snow and blizzard around the house as the little light sent shadows around Liz and her blanket. Placing the base back down on her mattress, she watched as the pieces slowly drifted down in the water. A wall of snow filled the world as it blanketed the house and yard in fields of unending white, a peaceful scene of her world captured within the confines of a piece of glass no larger than her hand.

Shaking the globe one final time, she ran her finger across the brass nameplate on the front, tiny words she couldn't read etched into the soft metal.

Krampusnacht

Liz had asked her parents what it meant, but her father had just shrugged his shoulders.

"There is a lot of old German heritage here in this neck of the woods. It's probably just what they called this area, but isn't it beautiful?" he had asked.

She didn't like that answer, but she had never been one to take "I don't know" for a response. Mother promised her that they would have the internet up and running after the New Year, and Liz swore to herself she would look it up then. It wouldn't be hard to get the translation off the computer, as long as they didn't monitor her too much. Her father had become particularly watchful of how both her and her mom used the computer lately, especially when it came to social sites where Liz met most of her friends.

"People don't need to know where we are at all times. We have no way of knowing who is watching us on the internet, anyone can see this stuff."

Her mother was always the first to disagree, but when Dad got stubborn, he always got his way, which to Liz had become more and more recent lately as the moving became more frequent. They tried to hide it from her, but they didn't always do such a good job.

He was right about one thing, though: the image was a perfect replica of their new house, and she loved it. Even Stevie had smiled when they gave it to Liz. Awake longer than even he should have been, her little brother had been all smiles and giggles as he helped her unwrap the new present. Bows and paper were his greatest excitement, and Liz was content on giving him the empty box after she took the glass out, the thin cardboard quickly finding its way on top of his head to a room warm with laughter.

"Are you awake, honey?" Her mother asked.

Startled, Liz threw back the blankets and sat up straight in bed. The snow globe toppled over and rolled to a stop against her knee, the white flakes inside swirling in circles around the house once again.

"Oh my God, Mom, you scared me!" Liz answered, the pounding of her heart a thump against the hand on her chest.

"I'm sorry, I just wanted to let you know that breakfast was ready," her mom answered with a warm smile.

She had her light purple housecoat on and pink, fuzzy slippers. Liz was always amazed how her mom always looked perfect, even in the early morning with barely a hair out of place and a face that glowed like a model. She hoped that when she grew up, she looked like her mother. Everyone always complimented how age had not changed her even a tiny bit.

"OK. I'll come right down," Liz said before she picked up the snow globe.

"I hope you really like that, I know your father spent a lot of time looking for it," her mom said. "Make sure you dress warm today. Your dad is taking you into town for supplies. We have a lot of stuff to do before Christmas gets here."

"I thought I was staying here with you to watch Stevie and set up the house?" Liz asked.

"Not today. Your dad wants you to go with him and see the area. I can take care of Stevie just fine, plus I could use some time to relax. It has been a big switch for all of us. Now hurry up before breakfast gets cold."

With a quick turn, Liz watched as her mom's house coat swirled like a 50's dress and she disappeared back down the stairs. She left the light smell of lavender behind as it mixed in with the warm embrace of buttermilk and bacon her father had filled the house with. Liz placed the globe back in the alcove before she rolled out of bed. The wood floor was as cold as ice. With a shiver, she reached for her suitcase and pulled it close to the edge of her mattress. She was going to town, and if it were as cold outside as in her room, she would need to wear all she could find.

Chapter 6

"You have everything you might need?" her father asked while finishing the last knot on his boots.

"I think so. Is it really that cold out?" Liz replied.

"Nothing colder than usual. You'll grow used to it pretty quickly," her dad replied with a pat on her shoulder. "Plus, I'm ordering some wood for the fireplace. Can you imagine it, a home with a real, warm fireplace?"

Liz smiled at the thought. She had always dreamed of lying on the floor, reading a book as flames crackled in the background and left a soft warmth throughout the house. Brittany had always bragged about the winter cottage her family had owned; now Liz was going to see how it really felt.

"Don't forget some more eggs, honey. Also, Stevie needs some cereal," her mom called out from the dining room.

She sat at the table with a magazine in her hand and a spoon full of cheerios ready to feed Stevie once he was done playing with the pieces stuck to his chin. Her father didn't answer. He finished zipping up his coat and looked down at her.

"You ready?"

There was no need to answer, Liz could feel the smile on her face. With a spring in her step, she threw open the door and raced out onto the porch. It had snowed during the night. A new layer of white covered the ground and the trees. Limbs bent under the blanket of powder to where she thought they were ready to break. There was no telling the difference between the yard and the driveway in the sea of bright snow that surrounded them.

"It looks like we got more than I thought," her dad said, his gloved fists balled at his waist as he surveyed the buried driveway.

"Can we get out?"

Her father looked down the long path to where it disappeared into the trees. More than four inches covered the drive between them and the opening that led to the highway, far more snow than the Prius had been driven through before.

"You want to learn something today?"

Liz looked at her father. There was a bit of mischief behind his eyes.

"Sure, Dad," she answered with a thousand questions racing through her mind.

"If you can keep a secret from your mother, I know how we can get out of here."

The devious smile on her father's face warmed Liz from the inside as she always loved their secret games and she could feel that she was certain her father was going to let her do something fun.

"Don't you ever tell your mother, but if you listen to me carefully and follow everything I say, I'll let you drive the car until we get to the road while I shovel in front of it."

Liz could feel the excitement of her heart racing. She was actually going to drive the car. Brittany would never believe this.

"Yes!" she shouted and took off, running for the car.

Snow and ice crunched under her boots as bits of crushed snow lifted as her heels kicked into the air. Cold air burned at her cheeks as she stopped at the driver side door, the metal handle cold enough to go through her mittens and puffs of white steam pouring steadily from her mouth.

"Now, you didn't let me finish, Liz," her father said with a smile on his face as he drew closer. "First thing is first, you have to listen to everything I say. Driving is not a joke, and a car is not a toy. Do you understand?"

"Yes."

She was going to say anything she needed to if it meant she would be behind the wheel.

"OK, the first thing we need is a shovel, or neither one of us is getting out of here."

"There should be one in the trunk, Dad."

"No, remember we brought everything inside last night."

Liz looked back at the house. The distance she had just covered in a few strides now felt like a mile if it meant she had to go back inside.

"Come on! Don't we have another?"

Her father didn't answer. His look told her enough as his lips flattened to a straight line and his hands waited on his hips.

"All right, I'll be right back," she said. Her foot slipped on a small patch of ice as she rounded the front of the car again and dropped to one knee.

"You OK, hun?" Her dad stepped to lift her back to her feet.

"I'm fine, I'll be right back."

Her knee stung like crazy, and her pants were already cold against her skin, but she didn't care. Just get inside and grab the shovel and leave. Then she'd be behind the wheel of her first car.

Through the stiffness of her knee, the smile stretched at her dry cheeks as she climbed back on the porch. She didn't see the shovel near the door, so they must have brought it inside at some point last night. Entering back in the house, she couldn't find it in the closet that held the rest of their coats and boots either.

"I told you this isn't the right time," her mom said from the dining room.

Who was her mom talking to? Liz could see Stevie sitting in his chair playing with his cheerios, which he had managed to spill all over his tray and the hardwood floor below.

"We just got here, and they are around too much. I will call you when the time is right, do you hear me?"

Liz walked on eggshells as she began to cross the foyer and head toward the kitchen. Whoever was on the other side of the conversation was not making her mom happy, and she didn't want to be on the wrong end if it was something she wasn't supposed to hear.

"I'm telling you, Tony, just let it be for now. The time is not right."

Liz caught her breath as she ducked behind the entrance to the kitchen. Her mom was talking to this Tony again. Who was he and what did he have to do with her mom? She could hear her mother pacing along the dining room table, her steps heavy and creaking the floor. There was nothing but sudden silence from the other room when Stevie started talking to himself and his food.

With soft steps, Liz eased out from behind the wall and as silent as a mouse entered the kitchen. Maybe they left the shovel near the back door, and her mom wouldn't notice her. She could get out quickly and ask her dad about this Tony.

"Just give me a few more days. It is almost Christmas you know," her mom said.

Her voice was right behind Liz, and it set her heart racing. Startled, she jumped off her feet and spun around. Metal pans crashed to the floor as her arm swept across the counter top.

"I'll call you back," her mom said a moment before she came racing into the kitchen. "Liz! What are you doing in here?"

A dozen answers fluttered past her lips without response as she stood there like a trapped animal.

"Look at the mess you've made," her mom said before she reached down and started picking up the pots.

"I'm sorry, Mom. Dad sent me in for a shovel, and I thought I heard—" She stopped the words on her tongue.

"You thought you heard what?"

"I swore I saw a mouse run in front of me and I jumped. My arm hit the pans, and they fell. I'm so sorry, Mom."

The warm smile she had always grown up with returned to her mom's face.

"The shovel is on the back porch. I used it to clear some snow this morning while your father was making pancakes. Grab it before he tries clearing a path with his boots. He still swears that will work."

Liz stood up in time to hear Stevie start to cry. "Thanks, Mom."

"Have fun with your dad today. Hold on, Stevie, Mommy is coming right back."

The blue plastic shovel sat resting against the railing of the back porch, just as her mom said it would be.

"We'll be back soon, Mom!" Liz called out as she exited the house from the back and began racing toward the front.

What was she going to tell her father? Maybe he knew who Tony was? So many questions needed to be answered and she didn't know where to start. First thing was first, she was going to learn how to drive.

Chapter 7

996 State Route 8. Marc waited in his car, the dashboard stained with a decade of coffee and enough cigarette ash rubbed into the ashtray that the center console had taken on a gray color. Down to his last pack, he swore himself he wouldn't forget to get another pack as he watched the edge of the family's driveway, waiting to see if they'd be leaving the house today.

They had moved into the one house he knew by heart. It was Tiffany's house. Today was supposed to be his day off, but not if they moved to this address. Just knowing they were in the house, he'd never let it go, so here he was watching and waiting.

Tiffany's parents had left the month the State Attorney announced that they had been dropped as suspects. Marc wasn't so sure it was a good decision. He couldn't find one shred of evidence that proved someone else had been in that house. Only the parents and little Tiffany. Picture in hand, he could feel the pull on his heart as his mind slipped into the darkness that must have been her final moments. Murdered on Christmas Eve. Taken from the one place she should have felt safe, and butchered like an animal. If only they could have found the body, maybe he would have been able to find something that linked the father to the murder.

The mother was petite like Tiffany. Barely over five feet tall, she could never have killed her daughter and then disposed of the body like it had never existed. George, the father, was a brute of a man though. Over six feet tall and edging on three hundred pounds, the man was all bull and then some. Deeply tanned skin with darker eyes gave the man an evil appearance.

It didn't matter which way Marc looked at him, he couldn't find a way to like him. With a history of drunken disorderly and one DUI, Marc wouldn't have put it past the man from doing something evil in a fit of rage.

The paper bent with his finger as he rubbed it over the surface of the picture, the folds, and creases that came with age as familiar to him as the lines that marked his calloused hands. Years of hard work were scratched into his skin. White lines over forty years of brown tan read like a boxing match of the century, twelve rounds of pounding away without tiring. His hard life would catch up to him one day. Either his body would go, or his mind. The doctor at the clinic warned him it was going to happen sooner than later, but without concrete evidence, he couldn't take him off the streets. It was better this way. Without the job, without the chase, his mind would slip away into a fog of nothing. Marc didn't want to live that way, not like his father had.

Stopped at the edge of the road, he watched as the doors to the Prius opened and the driver and passenger swapped spots. The father was teaching the young girl to drive. His reports said she was all of twelve years old, and judging her appearance, all elbows and knees as she ran around the front of the vehicle, he couldn't see any reason to doubt that number. A smile crept across his face, the sight of a father letting his little girl grow up before his eyes left a little warmth in Marc's heart. There was good in everyone, somewhere, even if it was buried in a case file as thick as the Bible.

Switching his car into drive, Marc pulled out from behind the public bus stop where he had been parked, the wooden rain shelter large enough to block a city bus if it needed to. Things looked to be going his way this morning. There had been no way for him to know if they would leave the house today, so he had found himself sitting once again and waiting. All of his patience was now paying off as he eased the car onto the road, the sound of wet snow splashing beneath his tires trailing behind him.

Blinker on, he didn't follow the father and daughter back into town, deciding he'd start with Mom first. They were usually the more reasonable when dealing with pairs. Plus, the baby would still be in the house, making the visit more cordial and less suspicious. Piles of snow that reached halfway up his car door walled him in as the forest drive led him to the house he hadn't seen in two years. Tall and as white as ever, the Victorian house sat like an heirloom that had been forgotten with time. The blue shutters gave it a peaceful beauty against the dark green and deep grays of the forest. Stopping his Malibu over the only patch of shoveled out driveway, Marc took notice of the shards of wood that were scattered on the ground. With a glance up, he could see where it had fallen from up near the roof. Time took its toll on everything, even houses that hadn't been touched since the passing of the little girl who once lived there. Shaking his prescription bottle in his hand, he could hear the familiar rattling of the pills that kept his pain away. His coffee was cold again, and he didn't want to wait in the car and make Mom nervous. That was never a good way to start. Tilting his head back, he chased two of the pain relievers down his throat with the rest of the stale coffee, a mix of cream and bitterness that rolled his empty stomach. Exiting the car, he rubbed the heel of his hand into his temple; the drugs were taking longer to work than they used to. He would have to go see the doc after the holidays, even if it meant sitting on her damn couch and talking about his ex-wives for an afternoon.

Most of the windows of the house were dark as Marc approached the front door. Looking closely, he could see a single light on deep in the house, most likely the kitchen or dining room, the remainder of the interior hidden within the shadows. It was cold, and the wind was beginning to pick up outside as he put the cigarette in his mouth. The temperature didn't bother anything but his hands as he rubbed them in front of his face, careful not to drop the Marlboro on the ground.

Two stiff knocks on the screen door sent the bones of his hand screaming as he tucked it back into his pocket and shifted on his feet, the sound of footsteps inside loud and clear before the inside door was pulled open.

"Tony, if that's you," the woman said but stopped as she stepped back at the sight of Marc standing in front of her door. "Oh, I'm sorry, I thought you might be someone else."

Marc nodded his chin and gave a sheepish smile as he gave her no indication that he watched her stuff her cell phone into her pocket.

"Sorry if I scared you, ma'am." Marc tipped his black fedora and pulled his long coat tighter against his body. "My name is Lawrence, and I live just on the other side of those trees." He stepped back and pointed to the encroaching forest on the east side of their yard. Not surprising him, she didn't step out and take a look expecting to see a house through a quarter mile of pine needles and slumbering wood. She wasn't dumb. "I heard I had new neighbors moving in and I wanted to introduce myself. I've been here my whole life, and I didn't feel it right to not come over and wish you and your family a Merry Christmas."

Marc tipped his hat again. Playing the part of anything but a detective always put his nerves on edge and his lungs burned for him to light the cigarette, but he had to stay in control, so he kept his hands buried in his pocket. She hesitated, her eyes scanning him as he stood two feet from her screen, shifting from foot to foot in the cold. There was no smile on her face, only the cold, hard look of someone who was put off by his presence alone. He'd have to think of another way to get her to talk.

"Is your husband at home?" he asked.

A metal spoon bounced across the kitchen floor a moment before the screams of a baby echoed through the house. Like a switch, a friendly smile replaced her irritated expression, and she stepped to the side.

"Why thank you, Lawrence. Please come in, you just missed my husband leaving with my daughter. They should be back shortly; they are only heading to the market to put in an order for wood for the stove. If you could excuse me a moment, Stevie looks like he dropped his spoon," she said.

Well aware of his presence, she didn't turn her back to him until she was over ten feet away, then with a quick spin on her slippered heels she was in the kitchen picking the baby up out of his highchair. His sobbing stopped the moment he could put his arms around her neck.

"Please take a seat in the living room, Lawrence. Would you like a coffee or some tea?" she asked, little Stevie bouncing on her hip.

"No thank you, ma'am. I've had enough already this morning."

Marc could feel the rumbling of his empty stomach, churning the stale liquid. He really should follow the doctor's orders and eat better, but now was not the time to worry about what time of day he ate.

She returned a smile before sitting on the love seat opposite the couch. They hadn't spent much time unpacking with boxes still taped and spread around the foyer and house. Marc could see each box was labeled and put in its place. Given enough time, he figured they would be moving in for good. Maybe for once, the family wasn't going to try and run again.

"So, what do you do around here, Lawrence?" she asked.

Stevie slipped off her lap and began to make his way across the room, his eyes locked on the light as it came in through the front window.

"I'm a handyman around town. A little of this, a little of that," he said. His cigarette rolled between his lips and without thinking he took his lighter out of his pocket but left it in the palm of his hand. "There isn't much that goes on around here that I don't know something about. I guess that's what happens when you've spent your whole life in these parts."

She smiled but didn't respond. Stevie made a few noises that sounded like words, but Marc couldn't understand them, though the little one was talking to whomever he saw outside.

"Oh, please, we don't smoke," she said without it being a request.

Marc hadn't even realized he had lifted his lighter to his mouth. "Sorry," he said before he tossed it back in his pocket and pulled the cigarette from between his lips. "Old habit I'm trying to kick. They say they die hard sometimes. Hehe. Where are you all moving from, if I may ask?"

Mom settled back in her seat, her leg crossed over and her housecoat reaching just past the skin of her knee. Her eyes had turned to the ceiling before she looked back at him. "Down near DC. Robert was able to retire from his work early and with the money he inherited from his father was able to buy this place. A real steal if you ask me."

"What did he do? I would guess he's young to have such a pretty wife as you," he said. A smile showing little teeth crossed her lips. "My wife would kill me if she heard me say that, if she was still alive."

"Well, I think I would agree with her, Mr. Lawrence. I might not be as young as you think, but please accept my condolences on your wife," she said with a sly smirk on her lips. "My husband was in recruitment and contract dissolution. HR kind of stuff for a big firm. Helped make them a lot of money, so before the owners retired, they gave him a big severance package and here we are." She held her arms out to display the house he had already searched a thousand times.

"Momma," Stevie called out.

Marc turned to him, his chubby cheeks red as he bit down on a plastic green building block he had pulled from a box as tall as he was. Buzzing brought his attention back to Mom as she stood up from her chair, cell phone already at her ear.

"Hello?" she asked. "Look, my new neighbor just stopped by. Yes, Robert stepped out of the house. He'll be in town for a little, but should be back soon. I told you to wait till later. What don't you understand about that?"

Marc could hear the anger in her voice.

"I'm so sorry, I really need to take this call. Do you mind if we take a rain check on this?" she asked after placing the phone against her shoulder. Marc knew there was little he could do to say no.

"No problem, I don't want to be a burden," he said.

Lifting himself off the couch, she stepped to the side and watched as he made his own way to the door.

"It was so nice meeting you, Lawrence. Please feel free to stop by again. Robert and Liz would love to meet you."

"As would I," Marc said with a smile.

He wasn't more than two steps away when the door slammed against the frame.

"Look, Tony, I already told you once..." Her voice faded behind the newly locked entrance.

Marc held his breath, but she was too far away to hear anymore, and his heart had already started to beat in his ears. Mom wasn't going to be as easy as he thought. Taking a mental note, he made his way back to his Malibu. A fine dusting of snow already clung to the windshield. Glancing at the large poster window that looked into the living room, he could see Stevie's chubby face as the baby pressed his nose against the glass. The little ones always suffer the most. Marc shook his head. Getting back into his car, he knew he'd be back, and he'd be back soon. With a final glance, he could see the soft white skin of the little boy's face before it was swallowed in the shadows of the house as he backed toward the forest that had led him in.

Chapter 8

Puddles pooled on the road as the town of Portswell grew closer, the hum of the car's engine a purr that settled into the background. The snow had been cleared off of the main road during the night, and by the looks of how clear the sidewalks were, those who lived here had been working at it for a few hours already.

"Everything OK, Liz?" Her father asked as he made the sharp right turn that followed Oxbow Lake and led back into the center of town.

"Me?" Liz asked.

She had been replaying her mom's conversation on the phone through her head.

"No, the other daughter of mine sitting right behind you. Liz, I want you to meet Kelly, she looks just like you except paler and her eyes are rolled back into her head."

"Eeww," she replied.

Her father laughed as he reached over and squeezed her arm. "I'm serious, is everything OK? I know this move wasn't something we all wanted. I promise it is the last time."

"You said that the last time we moved," she replied. She wasn't really angry about it, though she did miss hanging out with Brittany already.

"They promised me this time. No more moving. The house is ours, and we are here to stay."

Her father patted her knee as they pulled up to the Center Market. Built out of an A-frame log cabin, sweet smoke lifted into the sky and left the smell of maple hanging in the air to mix with gasoline as they got out of the car. Flashing neon lights of Labatt Blue and Mega Millions filled the windows that pointed out to the main highway as a long, sloping ramp led to the door on the west side of the building. Piles of snow larger than she was tall were pushed up at the rear of the building, the snow plow less concerned with appearance than they were with moving on to the next parking lot.

"You want anything while we are here? Soda maybe?" her father asked.

She shook her head no. Something to drink really wasn't on her mind as her hunger was currently satiated with questions. Inside, there were several aisles of snacks and drinks with two refrigerators of beer that lined the back wall. The smell of hot-dogs and hamburgers already carried out into the room as she took a seat in the first chair they reached as her father went to the front counter.

Portswell was a lot different compared to the cities in California and a place like Baltimore. People moved slower and watched you less as you walked around. Newspapers were piled into a three-foot plastic bin by the counter. Even as close to Christmas as they were, the folded sheets were only about a half inch thick. She could remember the toy advertisements in Baltimore were thicker than that.

"Woohoo!" Men's voices shouted from the parking lot just before the roar of an engine rattled the table Liz was resting against.

Her father turned and watched as four men, probably in their twenties judging by their dark hair and unkempt faces, slammed the front entrance against the railing as they entered. The cashier shook her head as the four, dressed in similar camo shirts with overalls tucked into thick leather boots, turned to the beer coolers in the back.

"I'll have Harold call you in the morning. He shouldn't have a problem getting a trailer of wood up to your house if that car of yours could make it," the cashier said.

"He'll be fine then, though it wasn't me driving. This pretty one here did all that by herself, I just did the shoveling," her dad answered as he waved her over.

Liz pushed away from the table and made her way over to him. The laughter and commotion caused by the men at the other end of the store was becoming hard to ignore. She was hoping they would leave soon. The new customers made her nervous, and she wanted to be back in the car where she would have more time to think.

"Vicky, meet my daughter Liz."

"How do you do, beautiful?" Vicky asked with her hand extended.

"I'm OK, I guess," Liz replied.

She shook the woman's hand and was surprised by the firm grip. Underneath the tag that said Vicky, Liz could see where it said "Manager". The strong smell of cigarette smoke filtered around the woman and Liz tried not to wrinkle her nose. Heavy set and almost as tall as her dad, she guessed the woman was older by the number of wrinkles that trailed out from the corners of her eyes and the skin marks on her hands. Gray peppered her red hair, though the roots looked more like the color of her dark eyebrows than the red that she had dyed it with.

"You got any more Molson back here, Vicky?" one of the men shouted with his head stuck inside the cooler.

"What you see is what you get, Tony!" she replied before she shook her head and pushed a knuckle into her temple.

Liz stepped away from her father as her heart skipped a beat. Tony?

"Everything OK, Liz?" her father asked.

She didn't answer as she stood still and watched the men start digging into the snack aisles.

"You know how it gets near Christmas. Deliveries are harder to get unless you want to pay more, and I doubt you and those hooligans of yours have enough to pay for what you think you are getting. Now close that door!" Vicky yelled to the four men.

Vicky handed her dad his plastic bag of eggs and a box of cheerios.

"Forgive them. A bunch of kids who just moved into town a week or two ago. Spend way too much money on beer and munchies, especially this early in the morning. They must have forgotten their manners with their mommas when they left in that damn truck of theirs. You take care now, and if I don't see you, have a good Christmas."

Liz felt the squeeze of her father's hand on her shoulder as he tipped his hat to the nice lady. Beers in hand, the four young men began making their way to the counter with bags of snacks hanging from their teeth. Her father picked up the pace of his feet as he guided her in front of him, making for the door a little faster than they arrived.

That couldn't possibly be the Tony that Mom was talking about? Liz wanted to ask her father so many questions, but she didn't know where to start. The cold air swirled around the store as it whipped off the lake with enough bite that Liz had to pull her jacket tighter.

"We going home now, Dad?" Liz asked.

"Yes we are, honey."

A few flakes of snow drifted from the sky as they approached their locked Prius. The men's truck was parked right beside it with tires that reached the bottom of the car's windows.

"That your faggoty ass car right there, twinkle toes?" a young man's voice asked.

Liz and her father turned to see that two of the men had followed them out of the store. The one Vicky had called Tony was as tall as her father, wide at the shoulders and with dirty blonde hair like Stevie. His face was clean and young like the college boys she saw walking down the street from the University of Maryland every day after she got home from school. They didn't have the scars or small marks from years of shaving and sun like her dad did. His eyes were bright but narrowed as he walked toward them. His follower was inches shorter but just as broad. A hunting cap covered his head, though tufts of neck-length brown hair curled out from below the brim.

Protectively, her father pushed her behind him as he stopped moving and held his plastic bag of goods at his side.

"Come again?" her father asked.

"You heard me. Does that piss ass, faggot car get your flower power going every time you turn it on?" the man asked with a smile while his friend stepped to the side. "The electricity got you all hot and bothered? I always wondered if men like you could even please a woman, or do you prefer them young like that little one you got cowering behind you?"

"Now watch what you say around my daughter. We are only here to pick up a few things. We don't want any trouble," her father said.

With a slow step, he pushed her closer to the car, but she could see the skin on his hands go white from where he squeezed the grocery bag between his fingers.

"Nobody here wants any trouble," the man said. His friend had almost circled behind them now. "We only want some answers. You are new to town, aren't you? So are we. My momma always said it was a good gesture to welcome people to the community, but we don't like those who do things to little kids, do we, Alex?"

The second man chuckled but didn't answer.

"Liz, get in the car," her father demanded.

"Hold on there, little missy," the second one said as he scooped up her arm inches before her fingers got to the release buttons.

Water splashed up into the air and landed at their feet as the front tires of a State Police car dipped into the puddle that separated the main road and the parking lot. Liz felt the squeeze of the man's grip disappear as he stepped away from her and their car. Her father stepped back and positioned himself in front of her again as the state trooper slowed and pulled his car up beside the truck.

"I'll be looking for those answers later," the young man said before he patted his friend on the back.

They started climbing into the backseat before Liz could see the first trooper step out in front of the truck. Her father gave the officer a quick tip of his cap before he turned and unlocked the doors.

Miles of road had passed before Liz felt her heart settle back down to normal.

Chapter 9

Liz could barely concentrate as she brushed her teeth. Her father swore her to secrecy as they drove home from the store, telling her it would just upset her mother more than the move had already done. She could understand what he meant. It was going to be Christmas in a few days, why would they want to make Mom worry about rowdy town punks. She didn't know who those men were and neither did her dad. One of them was named Tony, though. She wanted to confront her mom about it, but how could she? If those mean men at the store would upset her, asking her about this secret guy writing her letters would definitely not make it any better.

The house was feeling more like home as they spent the day unpacking and settling in. Liz had spent most of the afternoon putting up pictures of friends around her room and spreading out her books on the bookshelf that was built into the wall opposite her window. She had an extensive collection already, and her father promised that he would build her a new set of shelves when the spring arrived.

Making the place their own provided some distraction, though she found herself keeping an eye on where her mother went. Did she have a reason to mistrust her mom? She tried to shake off the feeling that there were secrets between them. When would she have time to see another man anyway? She was always with Stevie and the moving never let them settle. It didn't matter. Liz tried as hard as she could to push the concern from her thoughts, but whenever her mom would move to a different part of the house, she made sure she watched what was happening.

Stevie, on the other hand, had played most of the day while they moved things around and was now fast asleep in his room next to hers. He slept most nights soundly, so she didn't mind that he was so close, plus being his big sister, she sometimes would be the first to wake up if he cried and she would put him back down without her parents ever knowing. What else were big sisters for if they couldn't take care of their little brothers?

Liz watched as the water carried the bubbling toothpaste down the drain.

She would have to confront her mother in the morning. She knew she wouldn't sleep tonight and waiting several more days would just kill her from inside. Her father would want her to wait, but maybe this was something he needed to hear. Could her mother really be cheating on her dad?

In the corner of her eye she saw the box that had started it all was still pushed into the corner with its flaps bent and closed. Replacing her toothbrush in its holder, she sat down on the floor and pulled the cardboard against her legs. "Bathroom" was cut in half as only the letters for "room" could be read before she pulled it open. The same cans of shaving cream and deodorant littered the inside as she began to dig.

It was amazing how much you could fit into a tiny box and how you didn't realize the amount of stuff you had until you moved from home to home. She was beginning to realize it wasn't a good thing to keep too many possessions. They were just things you were forced to carry every time you left, but she knew she could never leave her books. They were her secret little escape that she would never be forced to leave behind.

Spread around her feet sat more than a dozen different items when she finally reached the bottom of the box. Extra tubes of toothpaste, a half empty bottle of her mom's favorite Dior perfume and various other things, but the one thing she was looking for was not there. The letter was missing.

Could her mother have taken it out already? Why would she put all of this stuff back instead of just unpacking? Maybe she already suspected that it was discovered and tried to cover her tracks?

Liz's stomach cramped as she turned the box over and around. Did she dream all of this? But her mother was talking to "Tony" on the phone just this morning. She could feel herself getting sick. She was worried about something that could be nothing but her imagination. Tomorrow morning—she would talk to her mom tomorrow morning. She would know the truth, and there would be nothing to worry about.

With a sigh, Liz stuffed everything back into the box. She could hear her parents talking downstairs. They didn't sound as happy as she hoped. Their words were short, and they cut each other off more than normal. It wasn't going to be a good time to go downstairs. Closing the bathroom door quietly, she decided she could go to bed without a glass of water. As quiet as a mouse, she tiptoed her way down the hall to check in on Stevie.

Chapter 10

Liz looked deep into the glass as the fake snow swirled around the little house, her new home. Inside the tiny ceramic model, light burned from a lightbulb which sent its rays into the darkness, lighting up the corners of her room, and laid highlights upon her belongings that had found their new and rightful places. Shadows swirled around as the little flakes spun and flipped through the liquid.

Whoever had made this had done such a good job at modeling it after the house. The shutters, the wrap around porch, it was all perfect. She imagined if she looked deep inside she could see herself lying in bed just like she was now with the comforter pulled up to her shoulders.

Only the light inside her real home had been turned off, leaving the still unsettled house foreign and unnerving. Her parents' voices had quieted over an hour ago as she laid in her bed, awake with the covers pulled tight to her chin to hold off the night chill. She had heard feet making their way to Stevie's before tiptoeing over to the master bedroom. She couldn't be certain if there were two sets or just one. If only one had come up, she knew that the morning would be rough.

Neither of her parents slept well when they went to bed angry. Dad usually slept on the couch when they fought, snoring with the tiny green afghan they used for decoration wrapped around his shoulders. She had to stifle a chuckle at the memory of two Christmases ago when her mother had banished him to the couch for not buying her something. Liz never found out what it was, but she always assumed it had been important, like a diamond or another piece of expensive jewelry. Mother was always in love with new jewelry.

Liz had awoken just after dawn that day and snuck downstairs to get a head start on the new Hunger Games book she had gotten and found him on the couch. The blanket was around his neck like a scarf and thunder rolled when he breathed. She usually had to be as quiet as a mouse when her dad slept; he was the lightest sleeper she had ever met. Even Stevie could sleep through more noise than him, but that morning a hurricane wouldn't have woken him up. She was six chapters in and her mother had already come down to start coffee before he woke up. She never told him that she took a picture of him snoring. It was her and mom's little secret.

Light danced across the walls as Liz gave the snow globe another shake. It was such a simple toy, yet for some reason it already meant so much to her. Maybe it was the house. She could feel a connection to it, though parts of it gave her pause, like the cellar and the attic. She tried to ignore it, but like the questions about her mother, there was something that watched her from the shadows. It was only her imagination; she knew it had to be. Ghosts and goblins only lived in books, and they were always defeated in the end.

For once she felt like she was home, and no matter what happened she wasn't going to have to leave. Her father promised her that.

Thunk!

The snow globe slipped from her hands and rolled across her bed as she jumped up and straightened herself on her knees. Something had fallen on the floor of the attic, vibrating the ceiling above her head with small bits of dust floating down through the light, like tiny leaves in the air. Liz could feel her heart racing, each beat pounding her chest as she tried to calm her breathing. Why was she so jumpy?

Time passed like molasses in winter as she waited. There was nothing in the attic for all she knew. Her parents had forbidden her from going up there, and she hadn't seen them venture up except the first night. Her father had pulled the ladder down and explored to make sure there were no signs of rodents or belongings that needed to be removed from the previous owner years ago.

"Nothing but a few spiders and some spare wood planks," he had reported.

Liz wasn't sure she liked the idea of an attic full of spiders any more than ghosts or goblins, but her mom had assured her that they'd go up there and clean it up in the spring. In her imagination, she would turn the room into a little library with walls full of books and a couch in front of the circular window to sit in and read by. Her father hadn't fixed the shutter yet so there must be a wonderful amount of light filling that room during the day.

Settled that there wasn't anything else moving around above her, she rolled onto her back and picked the snow globe up and lifted it to her face. With a few shakes the snow was falling again, and the lights resumed their dancing.

Krampusnacht. What did it mean? Liz ran her fingers over the etched in letters before giving it another shake. Not knowing itched at the back of her mind like all the other questions she wanted answered. The dictionary she had kept in her bookcase over the last five years was of no use. The word wasn't in English, so there was no way of finding it.

Thump! Thump! Scratch!

Liz shot up in her bed and hugged the snow globe to her chest. The sound of footsteps in the attic stopped as fast as they had started. There was definitely something up there. Terrified to the point where she could feel her hands shaking, Liz placed the snow globe on the bed where it wobbled next to her, and she slid to the edge. The floor was ice cold, and goose bumps covered her arms as she pushed herself onto her feet.

Floorboards creaked as she made her way to the door. Most of her stuff had been put away, and her room suddenly felt empty and dark as she reached for the handle. The light from the snow globe still filled the room as she turned the knob gently and eased the door open, hoping it wouldn't make a lot of noise.

There was nothing in the hallway but darkness. With a tiny bit of light escaping from her room, she could make out the outline of Stevie's doorframe, the door wide open to prevent the air from getting too cold. The hall toward the stairs was a mass of shadows, she couldn't make out anything past the length of her arm. If there were anything there, she wouldn't be able to tell.

The house was silent. Her father must have come up with Mom, or she would hear him snoring downstairs.

With nothing else to help her, she shuffled her way back to her bed and grabbed the snow globe. She would only go down to the end of the hall. The noise was above her and not below, so there would be no reason to go downstairs.

Toy in hand, she reached out of her room and let the light push back the darkness. Everything took on an orange hue as she looked down the empty passage. Her parents' door was shut, the room quiet where it sat just before the stairwell.

Thump!

There it was again. Liz caught the globe before it fell to the ground and shattered. Her heart pounded so loudly she knew it would wake the entire house. How could they not hear that? The drums of her heart felt like explosions in her head.

Above her parents' door, the ladder that folded down from the attic was closed. Her father had tacked the drawstring to the top of their doorframe to help prevent anyone from accidentally pulling it down on themselves, especially Stevie as he had a habit of grabbing at everything with his adventurous hands when he was being carried. Liz straightened herself before she took another step out of her room. With her back pressed against the wall, she moved toward the attic door. There had to be something up there.

Thump!

"Eeh!" she squealed and wrapped her arms around the light.

Large bodies of shadow circled the wall around her as the footsteps stopped next to the opening that would lead down into the house.

"Liz, what are you doing up and out of your bed?" her father called out.

His voice didn't come from in his room. It sounded awake and without a hint of sleep.

"What are you doing up, hun?" he asked.

She watched as the dark figure made its way up the stairs from the foyer. Her father's dark hair lightened as he came into the light, his face stern, but his eyes soft as he looked at her, though she could see the lack of sleep in the dark circles that surrounded them.

"Is everything alright?"

"I heard something up in the attic," she said.

Her hands were shaking where they tucked under her arms, and she could feel the weakness in her legs.

"There is nothing up there. I checked when we first got here."

"I know you did, Dad. I couldn't sleep, and I swear I heard something walking across the floor up there."

His comforting smile returned as he placed his hand on her shoulder.

"How about this? I'll go up and check again. You stay right here, and I'll get a flashlight. If nothing eats me, will you go back to bed?"

"Of course, Dad," she said, though a chill ran down her spine at the thought of something eating her father.

Within minutes the downstairs was lit up as bright as day, and he returned with his silver Maglite flashlight that he always carried with him outside of the house. Pulling the attic door down as gently as he could, Liz watched him ascend the steps with the powerful beam of light breaking the darkness above them. He didn't go fully into the room. She watched as he turned his bare feet and sat on the top step.

"Nothing but the same wood planks as before," he whispered. "I bet you heard one or two of them fall on the floor. There are a few leaning against the wall. It seems like your mother can sleep through gun shots if she tried."

He shook his head to his own comment before he stepped off the ladder and shut the attic door.

"I'm sorry, Dad. It just really scared me."

Liz felt ashamed for being weak. Both of her parents were so strong, she could feel the tears pooling at the edges of her eyes.

"Don't you worry about that. We all get scared sometimes. Here, let me tuck you back into bed."

He led her back into her room. Without making another sound, she was back in her bed, and he was at her door. It always amazed her how he could move in the darkness so quietly.

"Good night my little angel. I'll be downstairs if you need anything."

He pulled her door shut and vanished before she could ask why he wasn't sleeping in his room. Her heart still raced as the shadows closed in. Exhaustion pulled at her eyelids as she hugged her pillow close to her body. It must have been the boards upstairs. That was a good excuse, and there was always a good explanation for everything. Her eyes fell closed as her mind drifted to questions of her mother and the realization that Christmas was only days away.

Darkness began to fill her room as the tiny little light in the toy that modeled her home blacked out, a shadow cast from within the model looking into the house it would soon claim.

Chapter 11

"What were you thinking?" Liz's mother asked.

The voices were loud, angry and just outside Liz's bedroom door.

"I didn't leave it like this," her father answered.

Liz pushed herself onto her elbows. What were they talking about? Cold air filled her room like it had the previous mornings, so she wrapped herself in her blanket and tried to listen.

"Then who did? You are just so incompetent sometimes, Robert," her mom said with a sigh.

"Look, I thought I heard something fall in the attic last night, so I climbed up to check. There was nothing but the same pieces of wood and spiders. One of the boards probably toppled over and woke me up. I closed everything before I went back downstairs."

"Likely story. And why didn't I hear this from inside the bedroom and you could hear it downstairs?"

Her mother was angry. Liz hadn't heard her speak with such a stern tone since her father stayed out too late celebrating Stevie's birth.

"You sleep like a log, Amy. God himself would be lucky to wake you up sometimes."

"Don't you walk away from me!" her mom shouted.

Stevie was crying in his room. The noise and voices had probably woken him up. Liz could hear her father's footsteps descending the stairs as her mother passed her door and went into her brother's room.

Why were her parents so mad? Easing herself off her bed, she slipped on a pair of light blue bunny slippers she had unpacked, then made for the door. With arms wrapped around her chest, she poked her head into the hallway. Reaching the spot where the attic door opened up in the ceiling, she could see the ladder that went up into the attic fully extended with the door hanging in front of her parents' bedroom. It must have been a sight when mom woke up. Open one door to have another swinging in your face. No wonder she was angry.

"And what would have happened if Stevie would have found a way up there?" her mother yelled from insides Stevie's room.

His crying wails began to match her volume.

Her father didn't answer, but she could hear his heavy footsteps on the floor below. She wanted to tell her mom that she was up when dad went up into the attic. He had closed the door when he was done, she had seen him do it. She kept a safe distance as her mother carried her brother down the stairs. Her mother was a tall but slender woman, but when she was angry, her steps rattled the ground like a giant.

"Tell me, what would you have done then?" her mother asked again.

Liz could see her mom holding Stevie and her father lacing his boots in the living room.

"Think about what you are asking, Amy. A baby."

"Toddler."

"OK, a toddler is going to crawl over the railings of his bed, then make his way out of his room to finally climb an almost vertical ladder into the attic. He can't even walk yet!"

"He can walk!"

Her father sighed and turned back to his boots.

Her father had a point. She couldn't even imagine him making it out of his room, let alone up into the attic with his chubby little legs and feet wrapped in footy pajamas.

"It doesn't matter. He could have done it."

Liz bit her tongue as she watched her dad shake his head. This argument was going nowhere, and for the first time that she could remember, her mom was making no sense at all.

"Well, whatever you think. I need to head into town and check on that load of wood. Do we need anything from the store?"

Her mom shook her head and turned to the kitchen. Liz wasn't even sure if she noticed her standing on the stairs.

"Take Liz with you. Show her around town. Give her something to do other than wonder around, stuck in this house."

"She isn't even up yet. Let her stay and take care of Stevie. She hasn't even had a full day in the house yet."

"I can take care of Stevie. Now, don't argue with me. Go wake her up and take her with you."

She watched as her mother stalk out of the foyer and into the kitchen.

"Liz, think you can head upstairs and get ready? I'll shovel any of the drive that needs to be cleared before we go."

No words escaped her lips as she looked around the corner of the stairs and into the kitchen. Her mother was already at work getting a bowl of cereal set up for her brother. Her father remained where he kneeled near the entrance to the living room, his shoes tied and jacket zipped but his face toward the ground. But he just said she was still sleeping?

"Ugh, sure Dad. Just give me a minute to get dressed."

With a quick look into the living room, she could see the snow drifting down from the sky, large flakes that fell lazily as if there were no rush to get where they were going.

"Please hurry, Liz. We have a lot to get done today."

Taking two steps at a time, she headed to her room and grabbed what she could that would keep her warm.

Chapter 12

Plastic scratched against ice and snow as Liz barreled out of the house. It had snowed again during the night, and the driveway was a stream of white where her father hadn't reached and a gravel black where the blade dug into the ground.

"The keys are in the car. Start it up and bring it back slowly," her father yelled to her.

She skidded to a stop in front of the car as he continued to dig. He was already halfway down the drive and shoveling like it was a race to beat her to the end. Liz turned and looked at the house. What if Mom heard him? She could imagine her running out of the house in her housecoat screaming for them to stop. Mom was never the fun one when it came to letting Liz grow up quickly, that was all Dad's territory.

Tapping on the keypad, Liz's heart picked up speed at the sound of the locks giving way. On the front leather seat sat the keys, spread out with her dad's spare flashlight hanging off the ring.

Easing herself behind the wheel, she ran her father's instructions through her mind as if he were still sitting beside her. Adjust the mirrors, check. Take a look at your blind spots, check. She could feel the nerves wetting her palms. It had only been a day since the last time she drove the car, but it was still so new to her.

"Start backing it up whenever you are ready," he called from more than twenty feet down the drive.

She could see his smile in the rearview mirror. He had taken his hat off, and white steam rolled into the frosty air. Pressing the ignition, she felt the engine jump and begin to hum. Her father had returned to scraping away at the snow with renewed vigor. He was going so fast he might reach the end before she even got the car moving.

Setting the Prius into gear, she pressed her boot on the gas pedal and felt the engine rev as the car rocked backward. Giving it a little more gas, the tires started to turn, the crunch of ice and snow loud and clear as the yard started moving forward.

"Nice and steady, Liz!"

She squeezed on the wheel and stepped on the gas a little harder. The engine was beginning to do more than hum as the car strained to move. Pebbles and dark slush kicked into the air as the sound of rubber squealing shrieked into the air.

"Stop!" Her father yelled.

Liz took her foot off the gas and felt herself rock forward. Her knuckles were white where she was strangling the steering wheel. She was sitting on ice; there was nowhere for her to go.

"It's all right, hun. We'll get it out together," he said.

He knocked on the window so that she would open it for him.

"Now listen to me, push the gas when I say so and stop when the tires begin to spin. I'll push, and we'll get this moving."

She watched her father step to the front. Removing his gloves, he dug his boots into the ground and pressed himself against the front bumper.

"Ready?"

All she could do was shake her head. What happened if the car rolled on top of him?

"Go!"

She hit the gas, and the engine roared. Black dirt kicked in the air as the tires spun.

"Stop!"

The car kicked forward the moment she took her foot off the pedal. Her father jumped back as the car rocked back to where it had been parked.

"It's pretty stuck, isn't it? I think we'll need some ice melt," he said with his hands on his hips. "I'll run in and get some. I left it by the back door."

Two taps on the hood of the car with his hand and he started walking back to the house. Liz relaxed in the driver's seat, calming her breath to let her heart slow. The sky was bright through the white clouds overhead, leaving it a beautiful morning with the slow drop of snow. Only the hum of the engine broke the silence as she took in her new home. White covered the slate roof and piled near the front wall where her father had shoveled the morning before. Icicles as long as Stevie hung from the gutters along the roof and porch, jagged and deadly like spears waiting for a victim to stand below. The blue shutters were stained with salt from the snow, a film against their sun-bleached paint.

Liz yawned as she stretched her arms. Two nights without much sleep left her tired. It would be a few more days before she was able to finally relax. Then she'd sleep until the first days of her new school approached. The endless nights of butterflies and nervousness would start all over again as they always did.

Looking through the windows, she could see into her living room. The overhead light was on, and the oil painting of the Rocky Mountains that her parents had bought on their honeymoon hung on the far wall. Her mother was probably still in the kitchen with Stevie. It usually took her at least an hour to feed him. Cheerios were both his breakfast and one of his favorite toys.

Another yawn pulled at her lungs as she stretched again. Maybe she could catch a nap on the way to town, it took half an hour just to reach the center store. Eyelids half closed, she could feel her head begin to dip when the hairs on her arms stuck up, and goose bumps covered her skin. A cold chill ran down her back as dread sank deep into her stomach. The feeling that had scared her out of her room the previous night ran through her veins and burned in her blood.

She looked around and didn't understand why. There was no attic above her, and she was the only one outside, but the feeling cramped her stomach like the flu. White steam swirled in front of her mouth as she breathed out. The temperature suddenly felt ten degrees colder with frost building at the edges of the windows.

What is taking dad so long? Liz rubbed at her arms before she turned the knob to crank the heat of the car up. She could feel the air, but it was still bitter cold against her skin. Blowing hot breath into her mittened hands, she rubbed her palms together in front of her face.

Horror left her mind blank as she turned her attention away from the front door and back to the windows of the house. Dark, broad shoulders filled all but the top corners, the figure larger than even her father would be if he leaned against the frame. Red eyes, as deep as rubies, burned from a pair of eyes as it looked through the glass and left its gaze upon her. It didn't move, its attention locked on her as if trying to read her from across the yard, and then it turned toward the foyer.

Blood froze within her as she stared at the shadow, waiting for it to move. Not a single thought of what she should do would spring to life in her empty mind. With a slow step, the figured moved forward, its chest and body as thick as a barrel. Long, dark hair swayed behind it as it approached slow and steady with no rush in its step. On top of its head sat a helmet, one that reminded her of the Viking she had read about in history class with its horns like a bull.

Liz didn't know what to do. The stranger was almost to the foyer and would soon reach her mother and Stevie in the kitchen. Where was her dad? Ice cold sweat ran down her forehead as she screamed, but it wasn't loud enough. They couldn't hear her in the house. Shaking the steering wheel, she could feel the weakness of fear flow through her body. She was paralyzed where she sat, and he was almost to the next room.

HONK!

Her elbow hit the horn.

HONK! HONK!

The Prius' horn blared into the morning air as she hit it until her hand started to throb. The dark figure stopped moving and turned back to her. Its eyes flashed a blinding red as the noise filled their little forest alcove.

"What's wrong, Liz?" her father screamed as he came charging around the front porch.

Ice melt scattered across the front steps as he cleared them in a short jump. Feeling returned to her legs as she pushed with everything she could and stumbled out of the car, her foot slipping on ice and sending her to the ground.

"Someone's in the house! I just saw him through the window."

Liz could barely catch her breath. She pointed to the front windows as her father picked her off the ground.

"Wait here," he ordered.

There was a stern look on his face, one she had never seen before as he spun and ran toward the house. Her heart was pounding in her chest as the front door crashed against its frame when he threw it open.

"Amy!" he hollered.

"What?" she yelled back before she stepped out onto the porch.

Her housecoat was wrapped around her tightly, her arms crossed over her chest.

"Move. Liz says she saw someone in the house."

Liz watched as her father pushed passed her mother and turned into the living room. There was anger in her mom's eyes as Liz stepped onto the porch.

"So, you saw someone in the house?"

"Yes, he was in the living room."

"Did you see where he ran?" her father asked.

He stepped back into the foyer, his eyes darting from room to room. His cheeks had turned pink, but his lips were flat and motionless.

"No, I was too busy honking the horn. But he was standing right here!"

Liz stepped into the living room. Everything looked like it

was supposed to. Even her father's afghan was still folded on the couch.

"I swore. I really did see someone," Liz pleaded.

"See, take her into town. I think being stuck in this house is already getting to her," her mom said before wrapping her housecoat tighter and storming into the kitchen where Stevie was crying.

She watched her mom go, heavy footsteps shaking the floorboards of the house and rattling the frames that sat on the picture table in the foyer. Liz looked at the photos that sat on the tall bench, memories from their wedding and baby pictures of her and Stevie. They all looked happy. A steep contrast to the way her mom looked right now. To the side of her mom's picture where she stood dressed in a floor-length white gown with a train that went on for miles sat her mom's cell phone. The screen flashed with a countdown number on it.

Call Ended. 5:14 minutes.

Her father looked at her, his eyes searching hers before he turned back to the front door. Without a word he exited the house, leaving the door slightly ajar so she could follow. Liz returned her attention to the living room, her heart still racing but the adrenaline no longer in her blood. There really was someone, wasn't there? She took a final look at the couch and then through the front window. Maybe she had just imagined it. With a sigh, she looked at her mom, her back hunched as she fed Stevie another bite. She wanted to apologize, but her words failed her.

Chapter 13

"You catch that guy yet?" Officer Edwards ask with a chuckle. "Gonna sleep in that car of yours every night? Maybe we should just send your paychecks there. Detective Stutton, 1 Malibu Car, Portswell, New York."

Marc grimaced as the big man's hand slapped down on his shoulder as he sat at his desk. With more around his waist than he had in his head, the officer was fond of bad jokes and loud shows of attention directed at those who had more, knew more, or were the unlucky center of his attention. Marc had grown tired of the man's antics within weeks of settling in at the department, but Edwards was a fifteen year vet and well known even by those who didn't like him. A decade and a half and still a patrol officer. A career of speeding tickets and getting cats out of trees. His father had always warned him about men like Edwards, so lost in their own world, they don't realize everyone else has left them behind. They'll do anything to grab and keep people with them to ward off the feeling of failure. There were a couple in every precinct. This one happened to be 275 pounds and loud.

Turning back to the file folder he had opened in front of him, Marc ignored the next few comments that faded like the sound of the phone ringing at the receptionist's desk. The station had two of its five full-time officers in the office as Marc read through the reports for the fifth time that morning.

Robert and Amy O'Maille, suspected of fourteen disappearances, or murders, covering three states from the west coast to the Atlantic. It would have been easy to believe that it was all the father, dragging his family around as he tried to escape suspicion by moving around the country, but the mother was not like any other he had encountered. She was cool and collected. Marc's surprise visit had led to very little. He had thought he'd be able to rattle her a little, get her off edge and learn something that might be useful, but she was as cold as stone. That was until that phone call. Her voice, even through the front door, was enough to tell him that there were secrets waiting to be found. Maybe it was Robert, calling to check in, making sure no one had stopped by to ruin their cover. Whoever it was, Amy had not been happy.

Pictures scattered themselves across his desk, gray and whites of bodies that had been left in the open to rot. They weren't pretty, most beaten so badly the victims probably begged for it all to be over by the end. Six in California, three in Illinois, and five in Maryland. The trail ended on the streets of Baltimore, little to connect all the carnage except the O'Maille family; at least, that's who they were when all of this started. Marc wasn't privileged with the info that led the investigation to point toward them, the evidence circumspect from all angles, but who was he to judge? He did what he was told, and the fax buried underneath all the photocopies and typed dictation left little question what the department wanted him to do.

Follow with Caution.

He would do as he was asked, and this case had already taken a personal turn for him. Little Tiffany, so real to him he could feel her ghost standing in the corner, blood covered with a teddy bear in her hand, watching him. Her eyes staring and unforgiving with the bear's guts piling at her feet, dark and sloppy on the ground where it turned from white cotton to entrails and gore.

She was real, and he knew it. The doctor didn't know she watched him every night, in every shadow that followed in his wake, but the medication only helped so much. Migraines they called it, but Marc knew better. She needed his help, and he wouldn't ever give up the search for what happened to her. The killer would be brought to justice, or he'd die trying. His wife—no, ex-wife—didn't have the same convictions. She was gone now a year, and little had changed in his life. His job and his ghosts, it was what made Marc tick.

"Hey, I'm heading to the market, anyone want doughnuts?" Edwards called out, certain to sit on Marc's desk with the edge of his rump and knocking a few pictures to the floor. "No one? That's just more for me then. Catch you later, DETECTIVE!"

Marc watched with the corner of his eye as the man shuffled between desks, avoiding the phones that rang, and whistling at the receptionist as he passed. He'd be out until lunch, and probably bring back a ticket for some poor teenager while he was away. Real crime fighting, the community must be proud.

Cold, bitter coffee washed the medicine down Marc's throat, the pain now too much to handle as he began to sort the family's file. There had to be something he was missing, some clue he could use to approach them, regardless of what his superiors said. He wasn't going to let another set of killers leave that house while he was on watch, not this time.

Stuffing the medicine bottle back into his top drawer, he noticed he still had the faded green file folder that held the history of the old Victorian tucked inside—little Tiffany's family, and six other families that had moved in and out of Portswell since it was built in the late 1800s.

Clearing a spot on top of his coffee-stained calendar, a brown ring over the twenty-seventh of November, Marc shook his head as he swore to himself he'd fix the date when he was done. Where was time going? The years seemed to go by without changing, one day of pain and failure after another.

The first few pages contained pictures of the entire interior of the house, five bedrooms when it was originally built. He leafed through the photos, faded and yellowed with age as the reconstruction was documented back in the mid-50s. Fire had torn through the house with only one casualty, the family's youngest son, Kevin junior.

New buyers had sworn they would build it better than it had been, and they did. Reducing it to three bedrooms, they had furnished it with a modern kitchen for the time, a full dining room, and an attic up top that could split for an extra room. Two construction workers had been hurt, one working in the attic, and a second on the roof finishing the chimney. No records existed if the accidents had been fatal, but tragedy would not escape the newest residents.

Marc rubbed the back of his head as he flipped through more police and coroner records. The family's twin daughters disappeared on Christmas Eve in 1972. Vanished without a trace, the bodies or any pieces of remains were never found. The father was convicted in 1975, insisting that he had nothing to do with it, only to die in jail seven years later when they found him hanging in his cell.

The family home remained empty until 2002 when Little Tiffany and her parents moved in. Marc patted his pack of cigarettes on the table as he stared down at the report. No evidence found other than that bloody shirt and toy. How had they done it? There was no blood in the woods, only what was soaked into the cloth and bear, so they had to have done it in the house. Marc remembered combing every inch, every corner, and every floor to find anything that would let him catch her killer.

Cold chills ran down his spine as he held the edge of the file in his hand. There wasn't anything else to look at. It was almost Christmas, and the home had a new family with new children living in it for him to worry about. He could feel her standing just behind his chair. He couldn't touch her, and she didn't speak, but he felt whenever she was close. The hairs on the back of his neck would stand on end, and he knew what she wanted. She needed to be set free. Until her killer was found, she would never let that house go.

The feeling faded when he closed the file. Faded green, it was almost as thick as the O'Maille's with almost as much blood draining from its seams. He wouldn't let anything happen to those kids, not this time, and not by these parents. Placing the paper back in the drawer, he took a deep breath.

Follow with Caution.

Good words to live by. Marc sat up straight and pushed his chair back. Shock surged through his body as she materialized before him. Her eyes burned into his, blood dripping from her light blond hair while she stood motionless, teddy bear clenched to her chest.

Marc rubbed at the pain in his head, driving his knuckle into his temple. She had never made her presence this obvious before. Always lurking in the shadows, her corporeal body now remained translucent in the fluorescent light from above.

"Hey, close that window!" another officer yelled out.

A gust of wind, bitter and sharp, swept through the office and picked Marc's pictures up into the air. Tumbling as they floated to the ground, Marc jumped from his chair to catch them before they scattered under the desks tucked across from his. Evidence in hand, he looked back and noticed she was gone. No blood pooled on the floor, and no one noticed the dead little girl who had been standing there.

Sliding his chair back to his desk, he picked up his coffee cup to swallow what remained and hoped the caffeine would push back the pain.

"Damnit!" he said, the bottom of the cup wet from what had somehow spilled over.

Another stain for his useless calendar. Maybe he'd get another one ordered soon. Ripping the top month off, Marc crumpled the month of November in his hand and tossed it into the trash under his desk, the paper bouncing around before settling on top of the discarded coffee cups and crumpled packs of cigarettes. Looking back at his desk, frustration boiled over as he pushed himself away, the legs of his chair scratching the floor before he turned and headed toward the coffee station. Soaking through the previous month sat another copper ring. Like dried blood it circled the twenty-fifth of December. Two days from now.

Chapter 14

Silence hung heavy in the air the entire ride back into town. Her father wasn't angry from what she could tell. If he were, they would have been discussing the matter the whole trip, but he only sat in silence as he avoided puddles along the road with quick turns of the wheel as if he were some kind of race car driver. The distance between them spanned miles and made the few inches between their seats feel like an ocean.

She could feel the thoughts churning in his mind behind his eyes. Questions that needed to be answered and comments that needed words, but they sat empty and void. Or was she the only one who felt like this?

"Dad?" she asked, her voice low enough that she thought he might not have heard. It wouldn't matter, though. At least she had tried.

"Yes, honey?"

"Is something bothering you?"

She didn't look at him. Her eyes locked on the dark trees and dirty snow as it raced past them.

"No, not at all. Why do you ask?"

She turned and could see the smile on his face. It was fake. There was no light behind his eyes, at least not the kind she always remembered and could see in the photos that filled the house.

"Oh, I don't know. It's nothing really."

"Tell me, Liz. Is something bothering you?"

She felt the car slow down, the engine's purr becoming quieter in the background. The highway was empty, and the center of

Portswell was still several miles out.

"You and Mom have been fighting a lot," she squeezed out. Her heart was racing a mile a minute. She didn't know how she was going to ask him. "And it seems Mom, I mean I found..."

She let her voice trail off. Her hands were clammy, and she tried to look him in the face, but the thought of how angry her mom would be if she knew what she was thinking dried her throat out. She suddenly hoped they were going to the Center Market. She needed something to drink.

"You found what, hun?"

Liz took a deep breath. She ran the ideas through her mind, the letter in the box and the phone call she had overheard. What was her father going to do? Ask her mom about a letter that was no longer there, or about phone calls Liz had only heard the end of? She shook her head and let out all the air in her chest.

"It's nothing. I mean, I find Mom is a little different since we moved into the new house. She seems stressed."

Her father smiled at her, the warmth returned with a little twinkle in his eye.

"That's my girl, always looking out for the family," he said with a light pat on her leg. "Your mom will be OK. She's a big city lady and this is not exactly Baltimore or Los Angeles, but she'll come around. Just you watch, soon this will be home to her as much as it is to you and I. Sound good?"

Liz looked ahead. She thought about that answer, but couldn't make it quiet the questions in her mind. What other choices did she have?

"Yeah, OK Dad."

"Good, now I have a surprise coming up for you."

"What kind of surprise?" Liz answered, her frustration pushed back momentarily.

"It wouldn't be a surprise if I told you, now keep your eyes ahead, we'll be there soon."

Water splashed under their tires as they made the sharp right turn at the lake and entered the town. Snow laid itself in inches as they passed the center store and continued toward the west end of the village. Sidewalks were being shoveled, a few kids were out building forts and snowmen, and life in Portswell moved along as Liz pressed her cheek against the cold glass window on her side of the car.

"What happened at the house is bothering you, isn't it?" he said as he slowed the car down and turned down a side street with evergreen tree branches that reached across their path only a few feet above the top of the Prius.

Snow sat waiting for its chance to rain down on them, powdery and cold in their icy embrace.

"Uh, yeah. I think Mom is right, it's been hard adjusting to the new house, especially with Christmas and not having any friends around."

She was only half lying. The house had grown on her already and she only occasionally thought about Brittany. The celebration was still two days away, and she knew her best friend would already know what half if not all of her presents were and that's all she would talk about incessantly. A new iPhone had just come out, and Liz could guarantee that was one of them without even seeing the box.

"Don't you worry about this morning or your mother. This new home is going to be great for all of us. Just think of it as an escape. A place where we can all start new, make new lives for ourselves and be who we want to be. It's a clean slate, Liz. Not too many people get a chance at that. They only come once in a lifetime."

A new life? She was twelve years old. Why would she need a new life? She sighed again as the cold glass tingled against the skin of her cheek. It felt nice against the worry that warmed itself beneath her skin.

"There are some things I don't want to change, though," her father said as he slowed the car down and pulled into a ten space parking lot. "Here is my surprise for you this morning."

Built out of logs with a high steep roof, the building stretched the entire parking lot plus another half. Green shingles poked out from beneath the snow, and piles had been shoveled up along the sidewalk that rivaled even her in height.

"Where are we?" she asked.

"You'll see. I called ahead to make sure they would be open. Now hurry," her father said as he unbuckled himself and opened the car door.

Excitement jumpstarted her muscles as her fingers slipped on the release of her belt. She loved surprises, and her father always knew how to make her feel better when she wasn't feeling well. Slamming the car door shut, she raced around the front and caught up with her father in a few strides. He placed his hand on her shoulder as she wrapped an arm around his back.

"I was hoping this would make you feel more at home," he said as they turned around the largest snow pile that reached his height and was built next to the front door.

Portswell Community Library

Liz could feel the smile on her face. The small sign suction cupped to the door swayed and read "OPEN". With a pull, Liz could hear the air vacuum into the building as her father stepped to the side and swept his arm out like a chauffeur.

"Ladies first."

Her cheeks warmed as she smiled and walked through the glass doors. Single story, she could see that the entire library was one giant room. Reaching from one end to the other, shelves upon shelves of books laid out for her to look at. In the center there were empty tables lined up with lamps and scratch paper waiting patiently along the wood surfaces. On the far end she could see two green flannel couches that sat facing each other next to wall length windows that looked out to the snow covered yard stretching to the shadows that remained beneath the heavy limbs of the Adirondack forest. Burning maple filled the air and gave it warmth, the sound of softly crackling wood the only noise in the empty building.

"Can I help you with anything?" A woman asked from behind the front counter to the right of the door they had entered.

Liz could smell a hint of peppermint coming from the lady even at close to ten feet away.

"Yes, my daughter here would like to look at some of the books you have in stock," her father said with a smile.

He walked over to her and started discussing how they had just moved into the area and he wanted to make sure she had a card. He told her about how many books she could read in a week and how proud of that fact he was. Liz let most of the words fade as she looked up and down the aisles of books. This was larger than even the library she had frequented back in Baltimore. She could see herself spending a lot of time here. If her parents let her. Maybe she could make this a new home for herself. Every day seemed to give her new hope and new things to love about Portswell.

Dread sank into her stomach as the image from her house flashed across her mind. Those red eyes, and the darkness that surrounded whoever that was. The back of her throat went dry as she could see him staring at her in the car. Even across the yard she knew he could reach her.

"Liz?" her father asked, but the words were only noise in the background.

Her palms were damp, and she rubbed her thumbs across the clammy skin. Was he still at the house? How could Mom not have seen him?

"Liz, you OK?"

She turned back to the counter at the feeling of her father's hands on her shoulders.

"Yeah Dad, I'm alright," she answered with as fake a smile as she could muster.

"Good. Mrs. Beckler here is going to make sure you have anything you need while I'm gone."

Her eyes widened at those words.

"Where are you going?" she asked.

"I'm just going to stop at the Center Market and check on our wood delivery and run a few more errands. I didn't want you to be bored so I got you a library card and Mrs. Beckler promised you could read anything you like. How does that sound?"

Liz wasn't the happiest about being left behind, but she was at the library, and he was only running a few errands.

"I can handle that."

"That's my girl," he said before patting her shoulder.

With another big smile she watched him turn and leave the building, a determination behind his steps as he moved behind the snow pile and out of sight without the slightest look back at her through the doors. Turning back to Mrs. Beckler, she could see the kindness in the woman's eyes and the unfinished crocheting on the desk next to her. Shrugging her shoulders, Liz put her jacket down on the nearest table and started looking for something to read.

Chapter 15

"K. R. . ." Liz whispered to herself as she ran her finger over the edges of book spines.

Dust tickled her nose as she worked her way along the book shelves. Some edges, judging by the age and resistance they gave when she pulled on them, had been there for years without a single soul touching them.

"Oh, here it is!" Liz said to herself, loud enough for Mrs. Beckler to look up from her seat.

She was a nice enough woman. Thirty years had passed since she became the town's librarian and these books and shelves and empty tables were as close to a real family as she had ever had.

"Men don't understand a woman who finds more friendship and enjoyment from a book of board and paper than they do that thing that dangles between their legs," Mrs. Beckler had said while waving one wrinkly finger in the air.

Liz's cheeks had been on fire for what felt like twenty minutes after the conversation had ended. She liked boys and all, especially Jason who had been the top of her seventh-grade class, but that was all he was, a boy. She knew enough even at twelve that she was too young for that distraction, something that both her mom and her father had repeated more times than she could count. It hadn't stopped Jason from kissing her during the winter ball last year, though.

Liz wiped her arm across her lips after she sat down at the first available table. The tingles that had tickled her lips that night still lingered in her memory.

Christmas Legends and Other Holiday Myths

She opened the hardbound book to its table of contents. Yellowed paper with brown edges marked the inside and as she ran her finger over the gray lettering, dust lifted into the air from where it had shifted its way in between the pages over the years of neglect.

Krampus....page 295

It wasn't exactly the same name, but it was close enough. She had first tried to find an English to German dictionary, but there weren't any to be found. For a town that her father said had a large German heritage, there seemed to be very little when it came to German history or culture in what she could guess was easily a collection of a thousand books or more.

The paper felt as thin as tissue as she turned the page. Hand-drawn illustrations were printed every few pages. Little fairies and sea monsters, elves and enchanted deer told stories of creatures that had been the thing of nightmare for children over the last couple hundred years. Liz leafed through most of the pages, stopping to look at the pictures and to read the caption, but moved quickly on until she got to the page she needed.

Krampus

The name was definitely German. Its other spellings were words with too many consonants and too little vowels for her to pronounce. Paragraph after paragraph told her about old German stories and fables of St. Nicholas' secret helper, the one who joined him on his holiday adventures as he went into every boy and girl's house across the world. Except, when little Johnny or pretty little Sally were not on the "good" list, instead of leaving a stocking full of coal, Krampus was there to punish the bad children and set them straight so that next year St. Nicholas would find them on the correct list. There were descriptions of spankings and other undesired gifts being left, but very little else as she leafed through the pictures.

Discouraged, Liz considered going up to Mrs. Beckler for

help. If she had been the librarian for more than thirty years, she would surely know where there would be more information. No internet had been built out to this part of town, so residents had to look up any information they needed the old fashion way. Judging by the size of the card catalog and Mrs. Beckler's pride in displaying the polished cabinet and handwritten notes, Liz figured that was the way the older woman preferred it.

Liz sighed. Chin in her hand, she leafed through the next few pages on Krampus. None of this explained what the name Krampusnacht meant. She was almost to page 363 when her heart skipped a beat, and her arm pulled her hand away as if she had placed it on a hot stove.

"Are you OK over there, honey?" Mrs. Beckler asked.

Looking up in surprise, Liz hadn't realized she had gasped loud enough that the old librarian had noticed.

"Ugh, yeah, I'm OK," Liz lied.

Her heart was racing as she looked at the fading paper that marked the end of the book's chapter. Hand-drawn from old stories and claimed sightings stood a dark figure with broad shoulders, thick arms and dark hair that ran down its back. Sharp claws marked its hands and feet, horns like a Viking's helmet rose from its forehead. Eyes like fire, described in the caption as red as the fires of hell, burned into Liz from the paper itself.

It was him!

That was who she had seen. Goosebumps ran up and down her arms as her throat felt dry and she no longer had the strength to lift herself from her chair. How could she have seen him in her house? She had never heard of this Krampus before and what would he be doing in her house?

Turning back to the beginning of the chapter, she read and memorized every last word from front to back. There was so little to go on, and it all went back to old German folklore that had been around for centuries but long forgotten after the coming of Christianity. On shaky legs, Liz pushed herself away from the table and made her way back to the card catalog. There had to be more, and she was going to find it. Only two hours remained before her dad had to return or the library would close with her in it, and she wanted to know as much as she could.

Leafing through the neatly filed notecards, there was very little else she could find on her second trip to the cabinet. Why wasn't there anything here? Where had her father gotten that snow globe? Liz pushed the drawer shut, the slap of the wood loud enough to disturb all of the people who weren't in the library today.

"Is there anything I can help you find? It's Liz, isn't it?" Mrs. Beckler asked before she put down her half-completed new set of mittens.

"I don't know," Liz could feel the frustration in her answer.

"Here, honey. Let me see what I can help you find."

Liz stepped away from the cabinet. She eyed the closed book on the table she had been sitting at, then the woman who was now half way to her.

"I'm trying to find out the meaning of something that was engraved into a gift my father gave me. I think it's German and I can't read it," Liz said, a sudden feeling of sorrow taking over the frustration of having to ask for help.

"What did it say? My grandmother was German, you know. She used to tell me all about her time in Europe. I even visited once, but that was years after the wars."

"Krampus snatch," Liz said, but she knew immediately she had said it wrong.

The feeling of the words as they rolled from her lips never felt right.

Mrs. Beckler stopped with the cabinet between them and put her hand on the top as if looking for support. "What did you say?"

Liz repeated it, but she was pretty sure it sounded more like "Kram piss hatch", which she also knew wasn't right. Mrs. Beckler's face had turned a shade of gray as the legs of the card catalog groaned with the new weight being pressed against it.

"Come over to my desk, and you can write down what it is," the librarian said.

Liz wanted to ask if she was OK, but a wave of the woman's hand held her tongue as they both moved slowly toward the front of the library. Something in the way Mrs. Beckler was acting didn't feel right to Liz as she watched her drop herself into her chair. Crochet needles and yarn fell to the floor, but she didn't bother to pick them up. Instead, she turned to one of her desk drawers and opened it up. Removing a single paper tablet and pen, she slid it across the surface to Liz's hands.

"Go ahead and write it down the best you can remember the spelling," the woman said.

The pen shook in Liz's hand as she scratched out the letters. She couldn't say it, but she definitely could remember the spelling. Her fingers had traced the outline of that snow globe more than a hundred times in the last two days. She could feel every inch of it now if she closed her eyes.

"Are you sure this is what it says?"

Liz shook her head yes.

"My grandmother told me about this once," Mrs. Beckler said before taking a long, slow sip of her coffee. "Go ahead and sit down, honey. This might be a long story, and I don't want you falling over while I tell it."

Pulling a chair from the nearest table, Liz sat across from the woman with her arms patiently on the table. Sweat grew cold in the palms of her hands as she listened to the old German story of Krampusnacht. Slowly, the warmth of the world itself left that room as the story was as scary as she could have ever imagined it being.

Chapter 16

"Dad, where did you get the snow globe?" Liz asked.

Her father turned the car hard to the left as he put them back on the highway that passed through town and would eventually lead them back to their house. He didn't answer, his eyes locked on the road and his hands white-knuckling the steering wheel.

"Is everything, OK? You sure that door didn't hurt too much when it hit you in the face?"

His face was red and swollen beneath his left eye. Dark circles had already formed, and she could see purple and blue beginning to spread across his high cheekbones to the bridge of his nose. She leaned forward to get a better look. He said that the door at the center market swung open when he wasn't looking and clocked him in the face. The manager, Vicky, had been more than apologetic, even giving him a free soda and a bag of ice which now sat in the cup holder between them, half empty and not touched since they got in the car. Imagining how much it hurt just looking at his face, a drink didn't seem like enough of an apology. There would be no pictures of him again this Christmas, not looking like that. Her mom would be even angrier than she was this morning. They hadn't sat down for a family photo in four years and still didn't have one that included Stevie.

Liz looked off to the right of the road as Oxbow Lake passed by. Frozen solid, she could see the fields of white and blue as it stretched out to the horizon, the outer banks only visible where the water narrowed near town. Little huts were scattered across the frozen surface, a community of shacks that reminded her of the poor who used whatever they could to keep warm in the winter to survive on the streets of Baltimore. Cardboard and bent metal, tarps that were stained with age and flapped in the wind as the men and women sat inside. Instead of starving and praying for their next meal under an overpass while sitting in the dirt and trash of the city, these fishermen were probably drinking and praying for their next meal to bite the hook so they could reel it in. She could see a few trucks driving across the ice, the lake frozen thick enough to carry even those.

What happened if someone fell in? She squinted to see if she could see anyone walking on the ice, other than the desolate shacks and those two trucks. The town itself had been mostly empty since their arrival. She could count the number of people they had met on her hands, a small number compared to the cities where those she had met so far would probably live in the house next door, let alone the whole town. Hopefully, it wasn't like this all year long. She liked meeting new people, and if this was going to be home, then there was no reason to hide that they were here.

"Did you find anything interesting in the library?" her father asked without turning his attention from the road.

She looked at him before she answered. His eyes were darting from left to right as he kept the Prius moving steadily toward home. She could feel a tension in the car but didn't understand why.

"Not much. They have a good collection of books there, but nothing that stood out to me. Mrs. Beckler had some interesting stories, though," she replied.

Silence hung between them as they neared the center of Portswell. She could see the high pitched roof of the center market, dark green with its slate and a steady stream of gray smoke rising high above the trees. Flashing lights, red and blue, drew her attention away from her father's silence and swollen face as their car was waved by. A policeman, dressed in a thick brown coat and matching pants, nodded to them with his cap as he waved them through. Liz pushed herself around the side of her seat the best she could to see what was going on. Three police cars and one ambulance were stopped around the large truck she had seen the other day. She recognized the oversized tires as they reached the middle of the doors on the police cruisers that surrounded it.

"I wonder what's going on there. Did you see anything, Dad?" Liz asked as the lights began to fade into the distance.

"What stories did Mrs. Beckler have to tell you?"

"Didn't you hear me, Dad? Were there police when you left the market? There are a whole bunch of them now."

Liz involuntarily swung around in her seat as her father took the sharp left curve that would lead them out of the village. Settling herself, she wiped down her pants as she straightened her seatbelt.

"Don't mind the cops at the market. I bet it was just some of those kids drinking too much. Now back to what Mrs. Beckler had to tell you," her father said with a voice that left her no room to argue.

"Not much, really. I asked her about the German heritage of the area and about that snowglobe you gave me the night we got here."

He nodded his head but did not say anything else.

"Well, it happens that Mrs. Beckler's grandma was German. Did you know that there is a Christmas Devil?"

She could see his eyes turn toward her for a moment. The mischievous glare from them and the small incline of his lower lip was enough for her cheeks to redden with the silliness of her question before he turned them back to the road.

"Yeah, I didn't either, nor do I believe in it. She says he's Santa's helper and legend has it he punishes the bad kids instead of giving them coal. Could you believe that? Santa working with a devil?"

"Some people deserve what they get," he answered.

"Maybe, but you would have to believe in Santa to believe in this Krampus. Krampusacht is the name of the yearly festival.

It takes place on Christmas Eve. That's only a couple of nights from now, you know," she said.

A smile curved her lips as they continued their trip toward the house. She could already see their mailbox, dull black metal with white stains from the salted roads and the big number 996 on the side. Liz watched the trees slow as they approached their driveway, the ticking of the car's turn signal matching the speed of her heart as they waited for their chance to turn.

"She wouldn't dare," her father whispered, so low he probably expected she didn't hear.

Liz pushed herself higher in the seat so she could see past the hood of the car, her arms straining to see what was bothering her father. Snow had fallen from the trees as the temperature warmed while they were gone and a new layer of snow covered the drive. The white powder laid more in clumps mixed with old leaves and needles where it had fallen from limbs that now found the freedom to stand upright once again.

"Who put those tires marks there?" she asked.

Large grooves wove in and out of the snow as they made their way down the drive. Much wider than the Prius, the markings of the rubber left a deep path that their car could follow with no trouble.

"Did you hear me, Dad?"

He didn't answer. His hands were wrapped around the wheel so tight she could almost see it straining to remain attached. The house appeared before them as the trees opened up and revealed the little alcove they now called home. The white snow was blinding in the sunlight as they drew closer, the eaves above them bare with new piles of fallen snow down around the base of the outer walls.

"When we stop, go directly into the house. If Stevie is awake, you take him up to his room and read him a story," her father demanded as he slowed the car. "Do you understand me, Elizabeth?"

Liz could see the fire behind his eyes as the car came to a halt. His cheek had a large knot underneath the now purple skin of his face and his left eye was bloodshot. She almost didn't recognize him with as much anger behind his eyes.

"Of course, Dad. What's wrong?" she asked.

Turning to her door, she pulled on the release to let herself out. She could see where the large tires dug deep into the unshoveled snow and made its way around the house. It looked like the vehicle had gone around back, but who was it?

"Hurry now, Liz. Do what I said," her father demanded before he slammed the door to the car.

Shutting the door behind her, Liz ran to the front door, the wet crunch of snow beneath her boots as she reached the porch and bounded up the blue steps. Inside, she could hear her mother humming in the dining room, a soft melody of old Beatles songs that Stevie loved to fall asleep to. Stripping off her coat and sliding off her boots, she tiptoed to the kitchen. If Stevie was already asleep, she didn't want to wake him.

"Mom?" Liz whispered as she poked her head into the dining room.

There she was, in a short purple skirt and white blouse. Her mom paced before the back windows with Stevie long asleep on her shoulder. Her mom smiled before she put her finger to her lips. With a wave, Liz stepped into the dining room and walked around the table.

"Can I carry Stevie up to his room?" Liz asked with a voice no louder than a mouse.

Her mom smiled and shifted her baby brother on her shoulders. Rubbing him between his shoulders, she lifted him off her and turned him so that Liz could put him exactly where he had been. Pacifier in his mouth, she could feel the warmth of his body as he snuggled closer to her neck. He always did like taking afternoon naps. Her mom kissed the back of his head before she turned to go.

"Where is your father?" her mom asked.

"He was walking around the side of the house," Liz answered with exaggerated lips and very little noise. "I think he is mad."

With a wave of her hand, her mother sent her and Stevie off before she straightened the buttons on her blouse. Her smile had disappeared, and her eyes had gone cold, so Liz knew it was time to go. If her father was asking her to stay upstairs, then there was going to be a fight, and she didn't want anything to do with it. She would put her brother into his bed and disappear into a book, or at least try her best until the shouting ended.

Chapter 17

"What do they say happened?" Marc asked as the ambulance wheeled itself out of the parking lot and headed to the hospital in Elmira, NY.

"The boys aren't talking. They've clammed up tight. Scared or angry," Edwards said between sips of a blue Slurpee. "A little alcohol might loosen their lips."

"I think they've had enough already," Marc said, the smell of beer thick in the air around the men's truck.

Two of them sat on the edge of the ramp to the central market, one with a swollen left eye and the second with a lip split wide open and nursing it with a cloth one of the EMTs gave him.

Marc made his way over slowly. A patrol officer he barely recognized stood next to them writing a few notes even though the men weren't talking. There was no reason to rush, it was better to make them wait. The pain was always more aggravating while you were stuck with the authorities huddled around you.

"So which of you wants to speak up first?" Marc asked.

No response.

Typical.

"Let me get this straight from our esteemed Officer Edwards over here. You two, plus your friends, now finding their way to the nearest surgeon, get into a fight with a stranger. All five of you, which none of you know who this fellow was, get more than you bargained for. He drives away without a scratch and here you sit, nursing wounds like a couple of beaten puppies while two of your friends are gonna spend the next few nights regretting they were born."

"We aren't saying anything, pig," the tall blond said, refusing to look Marc in the face.

Pig. That was original.

"And why would that be?" Marc sat down next to him on the ramp, placing his arm on his shoulder and pinching the nerve just below his neck. He could feel the man flinch, but his pride wouldn't let him call out. "He wouldn't have you scared, would he? Maybe realizing you and your friends bit off more than you can chew."

The young man struggled to look up, Marc's thumb driving deeper into his shoulder. He'd let the pressure linger for a moment longer. There was never a reason not to drive the message home.

"Nothing happened. A little scuffle between men. We don't want to press charges, and unless you are going to find something to charge us with, I think it's time for us to go."

Marc pinched harder, and the kid slipped off his seat and fell to his knees.

"Disorderly conduct, and I bet my friend Edwards over here can find at least one open container in that dented piece of shit you call a truck."

A nod and Officer Edwards smiled. Leaning too far to his left, the large man tipped and fell to his side, the aluminum of the truck buckling as it caught his weight and prevented him from falling to the asphalt.

"You son of a bitch!"

Blond tried to jump to his feet, but his eyes rolled back as his neck stiffened and he fell to his knees again.

"Keep quiet all you want. I'll find out what happened here, either from Vicky inside, one of your friends nursing broken arms for the next six months or a birdie who sings to me every morning," Marc said. He stood up and released the man where he knelt. "One of these nice officers here will find someone to take care of your truck. I think it would be a good thing for the two of you to spend some time thinking your decisions here through."

Marc walked toward the entrance of the Central Market. Blondie was swearing something and spitting as the cuffs were put on. It didn't matter. He wasn't going to get anything from those two. Young muscles with no brains. Never a good combination.

A bell jingled to announce his entrance into the store. Two older men sat by the front window, their coffees going cold, and two sandwiches sat untouched on their plates. Vicky scrubbed at the front counter with a rag, a look of frustration written on the roadmap of her face.

"Exciting day so far, Vicky," Marc called out.

"If you want to call it that," she replied. With a sigh, she held the towel at her waist and stepped over to the register. "I already told your men outside, I didn't see anything. There really isn't a good view from here."

She was lying. Why would she cover something up? Marc turned to the older gentlemen who had returned to sipping at their coffees.

"They didn't see anything either, did you guys?"

Both men shook their heads no and slumped their shoulders before going back to nursing their drinks.

"No one seems to have seen much today. Pretty strange for a town this small, wouldn't you say? Especially this close to Christmas."

"Holidays make people do strange things, even in SMALL towns like this one," she said.

Turning back to the counter, she started scrubbing at the coffee stain Marc knew had been there for the past two years.

"Well, those two boys are going to be spending some good quality time thinking, and the other two will be lucky to be out of the hospital by the time Santa leaves them a pile of coal under the tree."

Marc reached down and picked up the morning newspaper.

Christmas Storm Approaching

Great, as if he didn't have enough trouble as it was.

"If you happen to remember anything, Vicky. You know how to get a hold of me."

He slapped two dollars down on the side of the register before rolling the bundle under his arms. Eyes watched him from under two pairs of old bushy eyebrows before he turned and tipped his fedora to the men who sat at the window. Their heads turned quickly back to the windows and the lights that flashed outside.

Chances are he knew who did this. Blondie and the others might be young and dumb, but this time they hit more off than they could ever imagine. Soon the sun would be going down, maybe it was time to pay another visit to his new "neighbors".

Chapter 18

Stevie remained asleep on Liz's bed as she watched him silently. He wrapped his chubby little arms around an old teddy bear, which was over half his size and missing its left eye. It had been hers when she was that young, and now it was his. Its brown fur had grown ruffled and dark over the years, and it smelled of mildew and drool, but her mom said it had been in the family since she was a child. Her little brother now loved it just as much as she had, and it made her smile when he squeezed it tighter and kicked out his feet with their little toes.

Book in hand, she sat at the end of her bed with the light of a small lamp clamped to her headboard and bent over her shoulder, shining on her and Stevie. She hadn't gotten far in her reading, barely two chapters in the hours she had now spent in her room. The sun had gone down over an hour before, and the fighting had just stopped. Their voices and words had been angry. It took Liz over thirty minutes of lullabies and rocking to stop her brother from crying while her mom and dad carried on down in the living room. She could feel where the collar of her own shirt had gone stiff with salt from the tears that had run down her cheeks.

Silence hung over the house now. A dread as heavy as a winter blanket enveloped the shadows that filled their four walls. Something about another man had filled the angry curses between her parents. "Tony" hadn't been mentioned, but her father seemed certain there was someone else. It didn't matter that her mom had explained the other tracks as being from the delivery of the pile of firewood that now sat behind the house, stacked tall enough that even Liz could see it from the window of her room. Her father must have been guessing that her mom was hiding something, even before she had found the letter at the bottom of the bathroom box.

Hunger bubbled in her stomach, the pains coming and going with the thought that she hadn't eaten since the granola bar Mrs. Beckler had given her. Heavy footsteps could be heard down below, but not much else. She was hoping the warm smells of dinner would soon make their way up to her room. She knew her parents had to be angry, but it was well past dinner, and Stevie would be up soon. He didn't like going without food when he was hungry, and though she knew fights sometimes meant long nights, tonight felt like it would be the worst yet if they had to skip dinner as well.

KNOCK

KNOCK

The front door rattled with the pounding. Who would be at our door at this time of night? Liz pushed herself to the edge of the bed, putting one hand on Stevie to make sure he didn't wake up, and then she stepped away and began to tiptoe her way to her closed door. Heavy footsteps made their way through the foyer below as she opened her room to the hallway and stepped out. She could hear her mom greeting someone, her voice much sweeter than it had been an hour before with her father.

Sliding her way along the wall, Liz looked down the stairs to the light below. A man older than her father, but not too old, at least judging by the gray peppered in his hair, stood at the door with her mom by his side, waiting with his hat held in both hands. Smiling, her father exited the living room and reached out to shake the stranger's hand. Liz could see the dark bruises on the side of her father's face. Blue and swollen, she could see the black circle around his left eye and the blood was still visible from where she now kneeled at the top of the stairs.

"I hope you two don't mind. Amy here had said that I had just missed you when I stopped by the other day. Coming back home from fixing Mrs. Coiler's front porch light, I thought I'd stop by," the man said while he looked past her parents and around the house. Liz caught her breath as his eyes stopped on her. Melting backward, she slithered into the shadows, hoping he hadn't seen her. "I didn't have your number, and I was hoping I had missed dinner so it wouldn't be so much of a bother."

"Oh, never a bother. I'm Robert, and as you say, you've already met my wife, Amy," her father replied. "I do apologize, Liz our daughter, and son Stevie, are upstairs sleeping. It's been a long couple of days for both of them. Please, take your coat off and come join us in the living room."

Liz inched forward, hoping to catch a final glance at them before they disappeared where she couldn't watch.

"Robert, I'm gonna," her mom said while pointing over her shoulder to the kitchen.

"Right, you go do that honey," her father said before he patted the man on the shoulder. "She's making a nice snack for the kids when they wake up. Cookies and hot cocoa as kind of a surprise. She'll join us when she is done."

Grumbling rolled through Liz's stomach at the thought of cookies. The foyer emptied as quickly as it had filled, leaving her at the top of the stairs alone. Pots and pans began to bang around in the kitchen below, the sound of water splashing rolling its way up the stairs. Liz wanted to go downstairs and meet their new neighbor, but she knew she couldn't leave Stevie on her bed. He'd probably roll out, fall and bump his head. Then her parents would probably forget they were mad at each other and become mad at her.

Temptation itched at the back of her mind, though. Maybe she could go down just a few steps and still listen in on what they talked about in the living room. She would still be close enough to her bedroom if Stevie needed her, but she would also be close enough to hear what they said. Breath held, she took one step at a time down the stairs. Socks warm on her feet, she moved her weight onto each board slowly, doing everything she could to prevent any noise until she reached two steps below where the shadows would no longer hide her.

"Looks like you got one hell of a shiner going on there, Robert," her neighbor stated.

"Yeah, door slapped me right in the face this afternoon. I wasn't really paying attention and Liz opened it up and WHAM!" her father answered. But that wasn't right, she never hit him with a door. "Gonna ruin Christmas pictures again this year."

"You have a real habit of doing that, Robert," her mother yelled out from the kitchen.

"She complains about it every year as well," her father said with a small chuckle.

"Doors have a real way of doing that to you, don't they," her neighbor said, though Liz could feel the doubt in his words in her own ears.

"So you're a handyman around here?" her father asked.

"Yep, there isn't much that goes on around here that I don't have some kind of hand in. Whenever there is something that needs to be fixed, I'm usually the first person they call."

"That's good to know. It's always good to know who to call in a pinch. I used to do something similar to that, back before I retired," her father replied.

Liz pressed her back against the wall and slid until she was seated on the stairs. She could hear her mother in the kitchen, the warm smell of chocolate and sugar now watering her mouth and knotting her stomach. Cookies and warm hot cocoa weren't exactly dinner, but she wasn't going to complain. Her mom always made great snacks, and the warm, fresh chocolate could melt an ice age. Liz knew she should get upstairs before her mom finished, but she needed to listen for more.

"What do you plan on doing after the holidays, now that your family is settling in comfortably?" the older gentleman asked.

The conversation was beginning to bore her anyway, her father giving the same answers he always did. Later, she would want to ask him why he lied about her hitting him with a door, though she knew she would have to come up with a good reason to why she knew what he said. Her life in this new house was becoming a tangled mess of questions she couldn't ask. Why were her parents hiding so much all of a sudden? Pressing up on her knees, she turned to begin her way back up the stairs. She wanted to be in her room reading when her mom came up with the surprise.

Ssssss POP!

The light in her room snapped when she reached the top step. The hallway and her room shuddered in darkness and silence. Blankets rustled on her bed, and she could feel the dread push the hunger from her stomach when she imagined her brother waking up and screaming. He'd try and crawl away, ending up on the floor as there was nothing to stop him.

Hands out in front, Liz slid forward on her socked feet until she felt the far wall with her fingertips and began making her way toward her room. Her curtains were pulled down to help keep the cold nights out, and with no lightbulbs, she would be entering a void, too thick to even see the hands in front of her face. She could hear Stevie tossing on the bed as she reached the doorway. He was about to wake up, the end of his nap long overdue and probably hungry enough to cry out and bring both of her parents up the stairs.

Eyes wide open, Liz tried to see anything as she stepped forward, pushing her toes so she wouldn't trip on anything, and feeling with her hands and knees with every step. Emptiness surrounded her, the echo of Stevie's movements coming from every direction as the distance between the door and the bed felt like it grew longer with each step. Her throat tightened, her brother's chewing on his pacifier now almost below her, yet she still hadn't found the bed. What kind of bad luck would take the light out at night when she wasn't within reach? She said a silent prayer in her head in hopes that she would reach Stevie in time.

Soft cloths and the mattress bumped against her legs in the emptiness that surrounded her. Looking down, she still couldn't see anything, so she reached out with her fanned out hands until the cotton comforter ran between her fingers, and she could feel the warmth of Stevie as he rolled around the bed. Pushing forward, she found him pressed against the cool wall. Propped on his knees, he was using the window sill as a way to get up and look around, though even with sharp baby eyes there wasn't anything to see.

"Ssh, Stevie. Liz is here to get you," she whispered with a voice that said don't cry

Wrapping her hands around his body, she hefted his weight until it was settled on her hips and she felt him snuggle against her shoulder.

"It's, OK. Mommy is making you something nice to eat," Liz said quietly before kissing the thin hair on top of his head.

Sliding her feet to the side, she followed the edge of her bed toward the wall. The lamp she read by was the only light in her room, and she didn't want to carry her brother in the pitch darkness out to the hallway. Within three steps she felt her shoulder bump against the bookcase, and without even seeing, she reached up until her hand found the snow globe.

"Here we go, Stevie. Maybe a little light for us to see by."

She gave the toy a shake and flipped the switch on the back with her thumb. Small flakes of white swirled around the miniature model of her house, the ground at its base quickly piling with the floating powder of a perfect snowy Christmas. The lights burned brightly as they lit up her room. The windows of the tiny structure strong enough to cast away the darkness that surrounded her and turn her world into a fog of shadows and hazy yellow.

Hefting Stevie further up her hip, Liz turned toward the doorway when a dark shadow circled around the room on all four walls. Her heart stopped, and the hairs on her arms sprang up. She was still alone in her room with her brother, she could see that. But what would cause a shadow like that to walk across her walls? Lifting the snow globe closer to her face, she could feel where Stevie shied away from the toy. Either the light was too bright for his eyes or something else.

She tried to see through the glass within the windows, looking to see if maybe some of the snowflakes had circled the house, creating the darkness that had chased itself around the light. Inches from her face she could almost see the tiny bulb inside burning, the white pieces of plastic not large enough to even bend the brightness now burning into her eyes.

Her back slammed against the wall, and Stevie cried out as she threw the snow globe across the room. Something had walked in front of the glass and looked right at her. It was dark, and it was in her room, not the room she stood in, but the one that was identical in the toy. Water ran across the floor, and white flakes drifted over the surface as she cradled her brother in her arms. The light of the toy quickly faded with the dimming of the tiny bulb inside the house.

Thump!

She heard the drop up in the attic, and she squeezed her brother closer. Her room was almost completely lost in shadow once again, and she had no strength to get them both off the floor from where she slid down the wall and sat.

Thump, thump!

Heavy, booted steps rattled the ceiling above her. Her heart seemed to match the rhythm as it drew closer. It was almost above her. Stevie gripped at her neck, his nails digging in as an ice-cold touch ran down her spine. Scratching replaced the heavy pounding as it crossed the space above her room. She could hear the wood peeling, like a nail across dry bark. She was shaking, and her brother, if he pressed himself any closer, would soon become part of her, his wails muffled in the folds of her shirt's collar.

Without warning, the scratching stopped, the noise ending above the wall across from her, leaving a dead silence in the room and the thunder of her own heart in her ears. Was it over? She still couldn't move, the strength in her legs gone and the grip of fear holding her on the floor. As suddenly as the noise had stopped, two burning eyes appeared across from her. Red flames, angry and evil, burned as their gaze bore into her. They didn't move, only looking at her, and she could feel her mind slipping.

Her eyelids struggled to stay open, and her breath came out in hyperventilating heaves. In silence, whatever it was took a step closer. Darkness surrounded it, no light could break through its evil, and she could feel it reaching out to her, grabbing with clawed hands at her skin and clothes. She was defenseless. Her heart thundering in her chest, she could feel it on the edge of bursting. She wanted to scream, but she didn't have the strength. Her mind said to keep fighting, but her will was gone. She could feel tears running down her cheeks as she squeezed onto Stevie for dear life.

Then everything changed. Nails bit into her neck as her little brother gripped the skin between her shoulder and neck with his tiny little fingers. The pain, the realization she was still alive, brought it all flooding back to her. The darkness and those eyes were halfway across the room when she grabbed hold of the little strength that burned deep inside of her and she screamed.

Chapter 19

He was good. Marc could tell by how fluid Robert was with his cover stories. He didn't miss a beat as he transitioned from one explanation to the next. Retiring in his mid-forties had always been his goal and once he had something on his mind he never let it up. Some things didn't quite fit if you laid them all out in your mind, but Marc made a mental note of each as they traded tales back and forth and knew he'd come back to them later. Each person telling lies to the other; hopefully, both unaware that the other didn't believe a word being said.

Robert showed no indication that he didn't believe his handyman story. Marc had only lived in Portswell for the last few years, but having spent enough time looking through old files, he knew the town as well as any townie who had lived here from the cradle onward. Their new home was Little Tiffany's house, and that helped a little. There wasn't an inch of this building he didn't know, probably even some that the new family hadn't found yet.

There would be time to get to that later. He was here for one thing, and one thing only.

Follow with Caution.

There hadn't been any other instructions, but he had already added one in his mind. The last little girl who had died here still haunted him, he could feel her sitting in the back of his car on his drive over, but she wasn't here now. During empty points of their conversation, he had stolen a chance to look in the corners, darkened with shadow. He knew she had to be waiting. There hadn't been a day since her death that she wasn't there with the pain that split his head in half, and now his fingers ached, his twitch uncontrollable by his side, so he balled them to prevent notice. Heat split his skull, and it took everything he had to stop himself from pressing his thumbs deep into his temples to find relief in any way he could.

"You wouldn't happen to have an extension ladder would you?" Robert asked.

"Huh?" Marc replied, the words lost in a momentary lapse of concentration. The splitting beneath his skull almost doubled him over.

"Are you OK, Lawrence?" Robert asked. Shifting his seat forward, he reached a hand out to help steady him.

The world swam in Marc's mind, sweat wetting his palms as he ran his hand through his thinning hair. The headaches had never been this bad before. Flashes of light danced in his vision and his stomach curled before he felt the warm pressure of Robert's hand keeping him upright.

"I'm fine," the words stumbled out of Marc's mouth. "A sudden migraine is all."

His hands were numb as he fished into his pocket. He knew the pill case had to be in one of them because he would never go anywhere without a way to relieve the pain. He could feel the cigarette pack, down to his last two lights. His lungs already burned for the next dose of nicotine.

"Let me check with Amy, maybe we can get you some cold water or a wet cloth for your head," Robert said before he stood up.

Marc tried to tell him not to bother, it would pass in a moment, but his tongue wouldn't move, and his throat felt like cotton.

"Daddy!"

The scream that split the lies and the stories, the distance and fake personas between them, pierced the night like a dagger in the dark of a back alley. A little girl's cry for help, one so riddled with fear that the pain in Marc's head dissipated as if it had never been there and the color of Robert's face, swollen and bruised, drained of all color, and he resembled the dead walking.

"Liz!" Robert cried.

In two steps he was already halfway up the stairs, bounding toward the darkness. Pans crashed to the floor in the kitchen, Amy following in the footsteps of Marc as they tried to keep up with Robert.

"Honey, what's the matter?" Robert called out, reaching for the switch that would light up the hallway.

A flash of orange and yellow sparked from the dusted glass cover on the ceiling, illuminating the space between the stairs and the room for a second before shadows swallowed them whole.

"Damn light!" Robert swore.

Some of the fastest hands Marc had ever seen brought the father's keys out and flashlight on. A blinding ray of white burst into the darkness that filled the children's room, pushing back the thick inky shadows. Marc could see the bed across from them, but nothing moved. Liz's crying could be heard in the deepest part of the shadows, her body lost in the darkness that separated them from wherever she hid. Stevie's muffled cries were barely audible over her sobs, his fear far more controlled than his sister's.

"I'll be right there, Stevie. You hold on," Amy said, her hand pushing Marc to the side.

They were only a step away from the door when a gust of wind, strong enough to ruffle the collar of Marc's shirt, slammed the door shut in their faces.

"Liz!" her father cried.

A new scream, piercing the depths of Marc's eardrums, split the night from behind the bedroom door. Twisting on the handle, he could hear the metal release refusing to give as their father squeezed the handle to the point Marc thought it would rip from its setting.

"God damn thing, open up!" Robert cursed.

Marc pushed Amy out of the way as gently as a rushing linebacker, her shoulder hitting the wall, though she didn't bat an eye in his direction as he moved to separate Robert from the child's room.

"Let me see what I can do," Marc ordered, digging his hand into his pocket and kneeling to force Robert out of the way.

Liz continued to wail from beyond their reach, and Marc struggled to steady his hands. There was a small set of screwdrivers on his keys. With a few quick turns he'd have the handle off and they'd be in. Cold, damp sweat coated his fingers as they struggled to get a hold of the chain that dangled deep inside his pants pocket. He knew he had been in situations far worse, where life and death were only a split second apart, and now he was no more use than the little baby who cried on the inside. His stiff little finger finally hooked on the ring, and Marc yanked at the collection and tore a hole the size of his index finger along the side of his pants.

"Daddy!" Liz screamed before a large thud shook the floor at their feet.

"Hold on!" Robert screamed before he threw Marc to the ground.

There was no stopping the man. Marc had been in fights before, with men more than twice his size, but the speed and ease at which their father slid him across the wood floor and to the guardrail was like something out of a comic book. With a single step, Robert drove his shoulder into the door, and the wood splintered around the frame. The lock held as a large crack opened up from top to bottom, splitting the entrance inches from the handle. A second drive sent wooden splinters into the air and darkness rolled out from the room like smoke.

Thick and oily, the cloud seeped into the hallway, filling the gaps and pushing the little bit of light that followed from down the stairs away. The substance felt alive, and Marc watched it move along the ceiling. Cold, icy fingers tickled their way down his spine as the mass moved along, searching for something until it pressed itself against the corner and began to roll down the wall. Shoulders and old bones aching, he forced himself onto his knees and began to crawl toward the opening that Robert had created into the kid's room.

"Liz, where are you!" Robert cried out as Marc neared the door, still on his knees.

Silence hung in the air, and Amy stood by the door crying, her cheeks red and wet.

"Answer me!"

Marc finally pulled himself to his feet and looked into the room. Emptiness filled the room, the shadows fighting the ray of light that burned from Robert's flashlight, the same thick mass that crawled its way across the ceiling filling the air of the tiny room and refusing to give way. Marc couldn't see the kids. The beam showed them the books that had been on the wall, the empty bed with its comforter pulled and crumpled on the floor. Nothing else was present. Where were the kids?

"There, what is that?" Amy screamed.

As fast as Marc could blink, Robert's aim turned to the far corner nearest the wall that joined with the hallway. Darkness evaporated before them, but did he just see a pair of eyes looking at them? Marc rubbed at his temple, the pain of his migraine quickly rushing back and his knees weakening with the sudden onslaught.

"Did you see that?" Marc asked.

The words rolled like thunder in his head, and the pain made him regret ever choosing to move his lips.

"I'm…I'm not sure," Robert responded.

"Daddy?" a little girl's voice, weak and raspy, asked from the corner between the bed and bookcase.

A second child's wailing erupted the moment the light turned to them in the darkness. Stevie, his face red and clinging to his sister's neck, screamed like only a baby could, ear-piercing and full of strength. A wool blanket, thick and flannel, covered them where the large unpacked moving box closed them into the corner, hiding them completely until the little girl pulled it open and revealed where they were.

"Baby, it's gonna be alright, ssh," Amy said, hysterical in her rush to get to the crying boy.

Tears continued to flow down the little girl's face as her brother was pulled from her side.

"Liz, what is going on?" her father asked, her mother speeding from the room with Stevie tucked onto her shoulder.

"Did you see him, Dad?" she asked.

Fear burned blood red in her eyes, a horror so deep Marc had only seen it a few times in his life. Belonging to those he knew were grateful to be alive, he had hoped he would never see it in the eyes of a child again.

"Did you see him, Dad?" she asked a second time.

Robert stood above her, his flashlight searching from corner to corner, but he didn't answer. Marc didn't know what to say either, but he had seen something. Something that sent a chill down deep into the recesses of his soul, and for once in his life, he knew he finally felt true fear.

Chapter 20

Shivers ran down Liz's arms and legs, forcing her to curl up closer to the couch, her back trying desperately to sink into the comforting couch. Wood crackled as it burned, the flames new and fresh from where her father had started the fire. She hugged the thick blanket tighter to her body, her eyes heavy with sleep that had eluded her most of the evening and her throat sore from the screaming that had scratched it raw. Morning light inched over the edge of the forest and traced a line along the far wall of the living room, small bits of dust floating in the rays as the house remained quiet.

Her father, she could tell, hadn't slept well either. She could hear him rustling on the couch near her, stepping away several times in the night and making his hourly trip up the stairs. Her mother had claimed the master bedroom and sent both of them downstairs with blankets and an inflatable mattress in tow. Horror and nightmare forgotten, whatever anger she held for her dad was still fresh and unrelenting.

At some point in the night, lying awake, but remaining quiet, she took notice of her father's movements and followed him after he was too far away to see her. She could hear his footsteps as they ascended the stairs to the hallway above. Unable to sleep from the fear that still exhausted her body, but kept her mind running at full speed, she waited to see if he would go in and check on her mom and brother, but he turned to the room she now refused to sleep in. Broken door resting against the wall, the crack had split through the frame as well, leaving both the door and wall in need of repair. She could see the beam of his flashlight circling the room. He was searching, unwilling to admit he had seen the same thing she had seen, but he knew there was something there.

Their neighbor had departed shortly after Liz had calmed down, shivering from both cold and fear. Her father had wrapped her in his green blanket and stocked the fire as warm as it would go. Hot chocolate in hand, she tried to convince them of what she saw, the demon eyes and the hissing sound it made as it drew close. It was large, and she could barely breathe as it reached out to her. Only the falling boxes, heavy and still full of photo books and frames, had separated her from the monster. She had pulled the cover over her and Stevie after she had screamed. She could still feel the sickness that had gripped her insides as the blanket began to pull away from her grip. She had screamed and held on with all she had, it had almost succeeded when the door crashed open and her father charged in.

Neither her dad or their neighbor, Lawrence, said anything as they listened to her retell a living nightmare. Her dad's face was stone cold and swollen, his eyes focused as he sat in silence. Lawrence had been willing to say it was strange how they had gotten locked in and understood how it could scare such a young girl. He told her how his youngest sister had almost frightened herself to death one day when she had locked herself in the bathroom during a shower. He tried to make her feel better when he let her know he had nicked named her "stinky" for two years because she refused to bathe with the door closed until she was almost sixteen years old. It didn't work.

Liz knew he was trying to help. The man had a tired face, but she could see a kindness behind his weary eyes. He was smart, though. Something about how he didn't hesitate when he spoke made her feel like there was more on his mind than he let on. In the few moments he sat with her. He had become a greater comfort than her mother had been. Terrified herself, she protected Stevie like a mother bear with its only cub. Her father and Lawrence were forbidden from coming within a few feet of her, let alone her brother who clung to her like a second skin. Fear, hatred or something else hid behind her mother's eyes, and Liz could see it in the way her mom paced along the foyer while she told her tale of the monster or the looks of disbelief and disgust at how she had left Stevie alone for even the smallest of time while she went to the bathroom. They didn't need to know Liz had been on the stairs; they were already angry enough.

"Are you awake, Liz?" her father asked, his head poking around the wall of the foyer.

Purple and swollen, the side of his face was twice as large as it normally was, giving him a pained look, though his smile was genuine when he noticed her eyes were open.

"Yeah, Dad," she answered.

Pushing herself onto her elbows, she turned to face the front window and pulled the blankets tighter.

"Here, this will warm you up," he said before handing her a fresh cup of hot cocoa. "Scary night, wasn't it?"

He took a sip of his own coffee before leaning forward and letting his eyes trail to the snowy fields outside their house.

"I'm still not sure what I think," Liz said. Doubt filled her mind. Could it have all been a mistake? Inside she knew there was no way, it was real, and the dread that surrounded her heart every time she closed her eyes told her it was true. "You do believe me, don't you, Dad?"

The hot liquid burned at her tongue and soothed her roughened throat as she waited for his answer. Discolored skin moved, his teeth chewing on the answer before he pushed himself back into the couch.

"The monster in your room? There are a lot of monsters in this world, Liz. I've met some of them, and they really are scary. None of them though had red fiery eyes and could vanish out of a little girl's room locked from the inside."

His words didn't comfort her. She wasn't a little girl anymore. She knew what she saw, and she could feel the anger building in her blood, pushing away the doubt and fear.

"It doesn't matter what I believe," he said. Sitting forward again, he placed a firm hand on her shoulder and gave it a small squeeze. His warmth melted away the anger as she placed her cheek against him. "What does matter is that you believe it and it scared you enough to try and protect Stevie. Your mother might not see that now, but you did everything you could to protect him, even putting yourself in front of whatever it was you saw. That was very brave of you, and I'm proud of you, Liz."

Her cheeks warmed with a smile that stretched across her face. Silently, her father pushed away from the couch and walked to the window.

"Dad?"

"Yes, Liz?"

She didn't know how to say it, but she knew she may not get a better chance than now.

"Is there something wrong with Mom? She has been acting weird."

His shoulders slumped before he reached up and placed his hand near the top of the window sill. Her father still looked like a young man, tall and lean as if he were twenty years younger. Older than most of her friend's parents, he always thanked people for their compliments and attributed it to his job and dedication to a life lived with a wonderful family. Liz wasn't sure she believed any of it because she was always told he worked in an office and her family wasn't always the happiest. Especially since they'd started moving all the time.

She had distant memories of a time when they didn't fight, but that was before they moved east from California. Since then her mother seemed to grow more distant day by day. When Stevie was born they had grown into a family again, the love her father held for their mom evident in the glow that reflected in his eyes, but not long after her brother came home, their mom began to grow distant, even for her.

"Are you ready to go out there again?" her father asked.

"Out where?" Liz asked, the blanket now wrapped around her

legs with the heat of the fire filling the room.

Her father didn't answer. He kept his mouth shut and continued to look out the window. A few blackbirds drifted high in the air, stubborn individuals determined to stick out the winter when the rest of their kind had flown to warmer climates.

"Out into the world, their world."

She was confused. What was he talking about? He sighed before he turned back to her.

"Would you like to go get some breakfast?" he asked.

Liz turned toward the stairs that led to where her mom and Stevie still slept.

"What about?"

"Never mind them this morning," her father cut her off. "Stevie needs his sleep, and I believe your mom needs some time to herself. How about you and I go grab something at the Central Market. I've been told they have some mouthwatering pancakes."

Liz smiled, and her father did as well.

"Sure Dad, I just need to go—" Her throat went dry before she could finish.

"Don't worry about that, I grabbed some clothes for you while you were asleep. I might not have your fashion sense, but you haven't unpacked much, so you made it easy on me."

Her father wrapped his arm around her shoulders.

"Be right back," she said.

The clothes were folded at the end of the couch, and she headed to the first floor bathroom. She could feel the darkness waiting for her as she walked past the stairs, the shadows and gloom calling for her. Picking up her pace, she squeezed the jeans she held at her waist and slid into the bathroom with all its lights on.

Chapter 21

The office was empty save him and the captain as Marc sipped at his coffee. Steamy but bitter, he closed his eyes against the burn as it flowed down the back of his throat. He was usually the first in the office in the morning and the last to leave. Now that they were only two days away from Christmas, the other officers were making themselves scarce, hoping to catch as much time with the family before the small town fell into its holiday slumber.

Fire Marshal Determination: Accidental spark from wiring error/Human error

Marc dropped the report on his desk. The family's records were piled neatly at the corner of his desk, closed between the manila sheets where he had left them the night before. He let his attention drift to the untouched folder. This was his assignment, direct from the Department in Albany.

Follow with Caution.

Since he left their house the night before, he couldn't get what happened to that little girl out of his mind. No matter who her father was, no matter what had happened before they arrived in this small Adirondack town, there was something within that house, and it had scared her half to death.

He closed his eyes and let the heat of his cup burn into the palm of his hands. Red eyes stared back at him, evil down to the darkened soul that gave it life. Could he have imagined the same thing she did? That wasn't possible. The pain pinched at his palms, a relief from the numbness that was building in his head.

"Is that what you saw your last night?" he asked through whispering lips.

Opening his eyes, she was standing in front of him. Wet hair, matted with blood and dirt. Her skin was a sickly white, and a dark river drained down her forehead from the crack that opened at the crown of her skull.

"Whatever that was, that's what I've been missing, isn't it?"

She didn't answer. The irises of her eyes were as deep as black holes and the more he stared at them, the more he could feel his mind slipping.

"You talking to someone there, Detective?" The captain called from his office in the far corner, exterior walls made entirely of windows so he could watch all that went on within earshot.

"No, sir!" Marc yelled back.

He could see the man sitting at his desk with his flat loafers crossed on his desk and the holiday stuffed paper open in his hands.

Turning back, he wasn't surprised to see that she had vanished. Pain pierced his mind as tiny sparks flickered through his eyes.

"Still aren't much for talking, are you Tiffany?"

He opened his desk drawer and pulled out the medication. Three pills left. He would have to stop by the pharmacy before they closed for Christmas. If he didn't, he knew where he'd be spending his holiday, and he couldn't afford to leave the family or that little girl alone that long.

Flipping back to the incident reports, he began leafing through the recorded deaths that had taken place over the years. None of them alike: adults, children, strangers and family. All turned into ghosts for any number of reasons, the only constant was that house. His vision glossed over as a burning poured through his skull and spilled over the back of his eyes. The pain always worsened before the pills kicked in. He'd stop to get more the first moment he got a chance to step away.

"Not feeling well, are ya?" The captain asked.

Marc looked up at the old officer. Neatly trimmed gray hair covered the man's head, but he hid a slowly forming second chin with a "Just for Men" dyed mustache and goatee. He dressed better than the other officers on the force, his uniform always pressed to perfection and his badge shined to a blinding brightness.

"You don't want to wear yourself out before the holiday, Marc. It gets real quiet around here after the drinking ends," his commanding officer said before pulling the opposite desk's chair out and seating himself. "I hear you've found something to keep yourself busy."

There wasn't a reason for him to know, captain of the force or not. Marc didn't answer to him when given direct orders from Albany, nonetheless he straightened himself up before turning his own chair.

"I think you could say that. My father always taught me that idle hands do the devil's work," Marc said.

"Your father sounds like a smart man, but there are many other things close enough to the devil for us to handle out there," the captain said with a nod of his chin toward the decades-old files on the property. "Don't go losing yourself in the past, not when the present is currently knocking on your front door."

He pushed himself away from the chair and slid it back behind the desk.

"I'm not sure I catch your meaning, Captain," Marc said.

"There was a call for you last night, and we couldn't reach you on the radio. Remember those two fools you sent to lockup for the fight outside the market?"

"Yeah, what about them? A couple of young kids looking to start trouble no matter where they were."

The captain turned and began walking back to his office. He stopped two desks away and flipped his finger on a Santa Claus bobblehead.

"Merry Christmas!" the toy called out as it swayed and its hula skirt rocked back and forth.

"One of them says they want to talk to you. Asked for you directly, said he thinks he remembers who it was that smartened him up real good."

Marc pushed himself away from his desk and onto his feet. Finally, a possible chance to bring the father in, maybe even dig further into the mystery that surrounded their whole family.

"A migraine is all it was, Captain. I must have slept through the call," Marc said before he draped his coat over his shoulders.

"Just remember what I said. Don't go digging into the past too deep. You may not be able to dig your way back out."

The door to the captain's office slammed, and Marc watched him sit down at his desk.

Christmas Storm!

Dark lettering printed itself across the front page. Zipping his coat up to his chin, Marc pulled his fedora on his head and reached into his pocket. Two smokes left, looks like he'd need more of those as well.

Chapter 22

Three cells. Not exactly what Marc would have called a lockup, but for a town with more injuries related to deer than violence, he guessed they served their purpose. The front receptionist smiled at him as he displayed his ID, her attention barely pulled away from the "US" magazine spread out in front of her.

"Which one was asking for me?" Marc asked.

She returned a look at him that said she had no idea what he was talking about. He would have been surprised if she could tell him what decade it was, her eyes caked with bright blue eye shadow and her hair permed until it was almost twelve inches from her head. Her perfume reminded him of his mother, overly fruity and nostril clearing. Though the crow's feet that stretched from her brown eyes made her look just as old as he felt.

"Take your pick. They've been calling out any name they can think of. Drunken louts," she mumbled before turning the next page.

He flipped his ID shut and stuffed it back into his pocket. Damn, he could feel the lone cigarette shift to make room; he had forgotten to stop at the market.

"I'll show myself to the back then," he said, not waiting for her response.

The guard who sat at the door to the back wasn't any better, his eyes locked on his cellphone and his breathing shallow enough that he was dangerously close to sleeping.

"Uh, hum," Marc cleared his throat.

"Yes?" Officer Stewarts asked, one eyebrow raised from the

football highlights playing on his phone.

"I need to see the two you have stewing back there."

Stewarts didn't move until the football landed in the hands of some player and the phone stalled to buffer its signal.

"You are welcome to them. They've been chattering like two birds waiting for their cages to open. Seem pretty happy for a pair looking to spend their holiday wasting away in here," Stewarts said.

A head taller than Marc, but with less hair, the man's uniform stretched at his belt when he turned to unlock the cold steel door that separated the front reception and the cells in the back.

"Hit the buzzer when you want out."

Marc nodded and stepped in. Clean, unencumbered light gave the tile floor a washed out white appearance and the walls were blinding as the door slammed behind him. It took a moment before his eyes could adjust, forcing him to wipe away the tears that pooled at the edges.

"Is that another stuffed pig coming to tell us what bad boys we've been?" a voice called from the furthest cell.

Marc let the heels of his shoes click with each step, slow and deliberate. There was no reason to speed up their entertainment. They'd be stuck in here until they sobered up and smartened up if the judge made the correct decision.

"A little birdie told me that you two cluckers were looking to sing a song," Marc said.

Metal screeched across the tile floor as he dragged a stool until it sat in front of the iron bars that held the men together.

"Ah, Detective. It is so good to see you again," the one he had talked to back at the market said with a smile.

The young man's eyes had cleared up, the alcohol flushed from his system, and what remained showed Marc all he needed to see. Forest green eyes with a desire for mischief stared back through the cell, a mop of dirty blond hair laying across light eyebrows and a smile that said he had all the confidence of a man who knew he had the world by its balls.

"I wish I could say the same, but you dragged me out into the cold to sit here on a very uncomfortable stool," Marc said.

They sat in silence for a few moments, the blond reclining on one of the cots and the second pacing back and forth. Shorter, but just as stalky, the second's long brown hair shined with a half week's grease and his eyes raced each other back and forth as he wrung an invisible towel dry between his fingers.

"Tony, will you just tell the man," the second said.

"Be quiet, Carl, you haven't finished digging a hole in the floor deep enough for us to escape yet," Tony answered.

Carl's face went as white as the wall. His eyes stopped at his feet, and a look of horror fell across his features when he saw Marc had raised his eyebrow.

"Let me cut to the chase here, boys," Marc said, and Carl began his pacing once again. "My captain told me you were looking to talk. He isn't a man to be bothered with the antics of useless high school drop outs like yourselves, and frankly, neither am I. I'm here to listen, and you have two minutes before I leave you where you sit. After that, you won't see me again until you are in front of a judge."

Tony sat up with a smile. Straightening out the sheets of his bed, he pushed himself to the edge and leaned forward, his smile promising a conspiracy.

"I think I'm ready to confess my sins, Detective. I also remember the name of the man who started this whole unfortunate misunderstanding at the market," Tony said before Carl dropped himself on the other bed with a thump. "I do hope that Vicky inside can forgive us, it wasn't our fault. We were just minding our own business the whole time."

"Vicky is fine, and I'll send your condolences," Marc said and leaned back against the wall. "You have one minute left."

Tony tapped his fingers over his lips one at a time before he leaned back and let himself rest on his elbows.

"The man's name is Robert, and he's new in town. Real ass if you ask me. Drives an ugly faggot Prius. You really can't miss him. Tried starting a fight with my friends. I tried to intervene, but you see how well that went."

"Clearly you aren't at fault then."

"See, Carl. I told you the detective was a good man. He sees it just like we do, and he'll put in a good word for us with the judge, won't you?"

Marc stood up and slid the stool to the side with his foot, the metal feet screaming across the floor.

"The judge makes his own decision. Hope you have a good Christmas, boys," Marc said.

Carl started calling out in protest, but Tony just scooted himself further up the cot. Their story was as weak as a newborn baby and had enough holes to drive that damn truck of theirs through. He had what he needed, though, a reason to talk to Robert about more than ghosts that lurked in the shadows. Marc reached the end of the hall and pushed the button for Officer Stewarts to let him out.

Fire lanced through his mind, weakening his knees and forcing him to use the wall to steady himself. There she stood, Tiffany with her bloody teddy bear. Dark gore pooled at her feet as she stared at him, her voice silent, but her eyes digging in deep. Marc could hear the locks turning from the other side of the door. Straightening his knees, he reached into his pocket. Only one left, he'd need to stop at the market first.

Chapter 23

Mom's attitude hadn't changed much with a night's rest and a morning to herself. She walked with a permanent scowl, never letting Stevie out of arms' reach, and she stayed in any room that her father wasn't currently in. Liz tried to occupy herself reading a book, but the words and the story wouldn't hold her attention. No matter how much trouble the characters got into, it didn't compare to what she saw at home.

"Damn it!" her mother yelled from inside the kitchen.

"Can I help?" Liz asked, placing her 3D wolf bookmark between the pages. With a quick glance, she was lucky if she had read ten pages over the last hour.

"No, you'll just be in the way," her mom replied.

Liz stepped into the foyer anyway. On hands and knees, her mom was wiping up a puddle of milk, white dishtowel in hand and her light blue blouse sleeves rolled up to her elbows. Stevie was in his usual spot, sitting in his highchair with macaroni and cheese smeared across his smiling cheeks.

"Are you sure, Mom?" Liz asked, stepping into the kitchen, her eyes searching for the nearest paper towel.

"You heard me. Doesn't your father need help with anything, or is he gone off to be the Lone Ranger again?"

Her father had left the house over an hour ago. Liz could see the Prius through the front windows, so she knew he couldn't have gone far. He had mentioned something about looking for a pile of wood of their own so they wouldn't have to pay such steep prices for next year, but that didn't mean much to her. What would he do if he found wood? Drag it back to the house and cut it to pieces with a kitchen knife?

Liz shrugged her shoulders at her mom, whose cheeks were red with exertion or frustration while still on her knees and bundling the towel between her hands.

"I'll be in the living room if you need me, Mom," Liz said and turned back into the foyer.

Snow crunched, and an engine revved as Liz neared the living room. Who could that be? She walked over to the window. Faded black and with a few dents along the front, Liz watched as an older Chevrolet pulled up beside the Prius. She didn't recognize the car, though the front orange license plates said "New York". Maybe it was one of her other neighbors.

"Mom, I think someone is here?"

"Who is it?" her mom called from the kitchen, the sink water stopping a moment later.

Liz slid her way through the foyer and opened the door, leaving the front screen shut. Long, dark overcoat pulled tight and fedora on his head, she recognized the man from the other evening the moment he rounded the corner.

"It's Mr. Lawrence from the other night."

He must have heard her because he looked up and smiled, his cheeks red from the cold.

"Hi, Liz. Are you feeling any better today?" he asked, his face tight, though the smile warmed his features. Liz could see his eyes searching the room behind her.

"I'm doing a little better, Mr. Lawrence. Thank you for asking," she answered, remembering that her mom insisted on her being polite at all times.

He stood behind the screen and waited as her mother's footsteps approached from the kitchen. Liz watched as the older gentleman removed his hat and ran his fingers through his graying hair. Men always did that in the presence of her mom.

"Who did you say it was?" her mother asked.

"Hi, Amy. I was hoping I could stop by and talk with your husband, Robert."

Liz stepped back after her mom put a hand on her shoulder and placed herself between their neighbor and her.

"Is there something wrong, Mr. Lawrence?"

Liz poked her head out from behind her mother when he didn't answer right away. He turned to look back at the path in the snow he followed that led to his car, then tried to search around her mom. As small as her mother could be at times, Liz knew from when she got in trouble, she could block a door if she wanted to.

"There's nothing wrong, I just needed to ask him something about yesterday. It's been bothering me, and I was hoping he could clear it up."

"Well, he's off in the woods doing God knows what. I'm not sure when he'll be back."

He nodded his head in agreement but didn't say anything. Liz looked up at her mom who had turned so she could see Stevie in the kitchen.

"You could sit in the living room until he gets back. I'm sorry, I won't be much company. I have a lot of cleaning to do, but maybe Liz here could chat with you for a little bit. Robert will be back soon enough."

Butterflies jumped in Liz's stomach when the man's eyes looked down at her. As she saw from the night before, they looked kind and tired, yet he wanted something this time. He was here for a purpose, but she didn't know what. She could tell by how he continued to search, though he remained quiet. Hopefully, he didn't want to talk about the monster from the other night. She could still see glowing eyes in every corner and every shadow. When the house was quiet, even though her mother was in the next room, every scratch and hiss made her jump. She wasn't sure she was ready to talk about that again.

"Would you mind doing that, Liz?" Mr. Lawrence asked. "I hope your father will be home soon, but it would be nice to have a little company for a while."

Liz looked up at her mother. The warm smile was still on her face, but her dark eyes had gone cold. She knew the last thing she could do was say no.

"I would love to, Mr. Lawrence. I was just reading by the fire."

Nodding, her mom brushed passed her and headed toward the kitchen and her little brother. The eyebrow over her neighbor's eye peeked at the site of her mom closing up so abruptly, leaving her to open the door.

"Are you sure everything is, OK?" he asked.

"It's the day before Christmas, what could go wrong?" she answered, though the smile on her face was as fake as the story her father had told the man just the other evening.

Chapter 24

"Hey, Liz! Get your coat on, I need some help getting something into the house," Robert called out.

The little girl practically jumped several feet into the air as his voice bellowed into the house when the front door opened. The sound of stomping boots quickly followed as she raced across the living room. Marc sat back against the sofa seat and waited. How was he going to approach this? Robert was a dangerous man under normal circumstances, and who knew how he would be feeling threatened in his home. Would he even feel threatened?

"He's right in here, Dad," Liz said.

Her bobbing head poked around the half wall of the foyer and was quickly followed by her father. Dark purple stretched from eye to chin, the man's face was now only beginning to heal from the damage inflicted, and Marc could see small edges of green where the blood was fading.

"Ah, Mr. Lawrence. How good to see you again," Robert said with his hand extended. Marc took note of the bark embedded into the glove he still wore on the other hand. "What brings you by this time of day?"

Little Liz stood behind her father to the side enough so she could see and hear everything. Smart girl. Just like another one he knew.

"I have a few questions that came to my mind about yesterday. It's been bothering me, and I was hoping to catch you before the holiday. You know, while you might have a chance to step away."

Robert's eyes narrowed without a word passing between them. Marc could feel where his identification as a detective with the

Albany Person of Interest and the concealed Beretta he placed by his wallet hung heavily on him, but looking at the man in front of him, he didn't know if any of that would matter if this got out of hand.

"Sure, whatever you need, Lawrence," he said. "First, if you don't mind, I have a surprise here for Liz. Now that you are here, though, I was wondering if maybe you could help as well with it."

Pulling the cotton orange hat he wore tighter to his head, the father stepped back and put a large hand on the girl's shoulder.

"What do you have, Dad?"

"It's a surprise. You should come outside to see it. What do you say, Lawrence?"

This was dangerous. He knew Robert had to be on to him, the man was smarter than the normal street thug and definitely a page ahead of the drunks he had found over the last three years, but Marc couldn't find an easier path that would lead them both out of the house and away from the family. If he tried to end the charade here, with Amy and the baby in the kitchen and their daughter Liz by his side, this could grow ugly, fast.

"That shouldn't be too much of a problem," Marc said before he leaned down to the chair he had been sitting on. Picking up his hat, he smiled at the father and daughter who waited for him. "There isn't much I like more than a good surprise."

"Yay!" Liz blurted before she raced through the foyer.

Robert nodded with a look of suspicion in his eyes.

"Is it something you hid in the car?" Liz questioned as she raced out the door.

"Nope, I have it around the back of the house," her dad said.

Marc stepped outside when Robert held the door open for him.

"I do hope you don't mind waiting just a little longer, Lawrence. It has been a rough move this time for Liz, especially with her mother, so I didn't want to wait too long to do something that would brighten her day."

Marc watched as the girl left a trail of flying snow in her wake. "What is wrong with Amy? She seems distant today if you don't mind me asking," Marc said.

He knew he needed to approach this cautiously.

Robert shrugged and looked down at the trail of footsteps his daughter left.

"I think her mom is taking this move just as hard. I promised her it was the last time. I finished my last assignment down in Maryland and left that life behind. This is a new start for us, Mr. Lawrence. You ever needed a fresh beginning? Somewhere you could leave the demons behind you and welcome each morning with hope for a better day?"

Marc looked into the man's eyes. There was a longing behind the deep green color. Something reaching for a dream that was so close at hand, yet so far away.

Marc couldn't remember if he knew what that felt like, then a burn began to roll up from behind his collar, trickling just below the scalp. She was watching him, with those same dead eyes and that bloody teddy bear. He could feel her only steps away, in some shadow, watching them circle her old house.

"Daddy!" Liz screamed out.

Without hesitation, Marc steamed forward, his feet sinking into the snow as he rounded the corner of the house. Sliding on the ice hidden below the powder, Marc's knees ached when the little girl came into view, jumping up and down with her mittened hands covering her smile that extended from ear to ear.

Taking his time, Robert walked around the house and patted Marc on the shoulder.

"The other night does have you on edge, doesn't it?" he said, a bit of joy under the surface of his words. "I know it's a bit late, honey, but I found it, and I knew it was perfect. We can get it into the house and decorate it before the night is through."

Liz squealed and raced for her father. Arms wrapped around him, Marc watched as the little twelve-year-old almost took the man right off of his feet. A small bit of remorse filled the tiny space in his chest where he allowed himself to feel for those he knew deserved what they had coming. The feeling disappeared as quickly as the pain in his skull sent sparkling lights through his eyes.

"I can't wait to tell Mom," Liz said, jumping before she wrapped her arms around her father again. "Did she know you were looking for a tree?"

"No, she didn't baby. No, she didn't."

Robert hugged his daughter back before pulling her away and crouching down on his knees in front of her.

"Why don't you go inside and break the news to Mom. I think Mr. Lawrence here has some things he wants to talk to me about, and I bet he'd prefer to stay outside in such nice weather. Isn't that correct?"

Marc smiled and nodded in agreement as he stepped around wide to let the little girl have a clear path back to the front.

"Go on in and talk to your momma, hun. I just have a few things to ask your dad. It should only take a minute."

Liz looked at him, a curious question on her face with her eyebrows scrunched together, then turning she hugged her father again and took off running back toward the front of the house.

"So, what can I help you with Lawrence? You aren't seeing ghosts of your own are you?" Robert asked.

He took a few steps toward Marc, who backed up a step or two.

"Each of us has ghosts of our own, Robert. Some stick with us a little longer than usual."

The father closed his eyes and took a deep breath with his face to the sky when he reached the Christmas tree. Standing easily eight feet tall, it had to have taken a great feat of strength to drag that from wherever the man had cut it down.

His palm itching with anticipation, Marc let his thumb settle into the tip of his pants pocket, pulling back the opening of his coat.

"What can I help you with then, Lawrence?" Robert asked. He reached around the side of the tree, his hand disappearing before reemerging with an axe gripped tightly within his gloved hand.

"It's about that bruise on your face, Robert, and you can call me Detective Stutton," Marc said before he opened his coat enough to reveal his badge and ID. "I was made aware that you may be possibly involved in an altercation outside of the Central Market, and I was wondering if you would come down to the station and help me revisit that story of Liz smacking you in the face with a door."

Marc's heart raced while the father stood there, axe in hand and eyes as cold as the snow that surrounded him. If he raced forward, he knew there would be no time to withdraw his weapon; the man could clear that distance before his fingers ever found the holster.

Marc wasn't much of a believer in God, nor ghosts for that matter, though he was plagued by one that followed him everywhere. Pain pulsed with the blood that rushed through his veins; his breath held as the two of them stood silently looking at each other.

"What do you say, Robert? How about you and I talk about this privately. If it's as you say, you'll be home before dinner, and there will be plenty of time to decorate this tree. The family inside doesn't even need to know."

It was a lie, and both of them knew it. Marc had him cornered, and there would be no coming back. Robert let out a heavy sigh before he turned back to the tree.

"Detective Stutton is it? I believe there has been a big misunderstanding, but as you have graciously kept my family out of this, I think I will do as you ask," Robert said.

In a swipe that caught Marc by surprise, the axe bit half way up the blade as it embedded itself into the side of the tree's trunk. Throat gone shut, Marc realized that his hand had only made it to the side of his leg before it was all over.

"Are we taking your car or mine?" Robert asked.

Marc nodded for the other to take the lead. Heart pounding and head screaming, he took a deep breath before he turned to follow, his eyes lingering on the man's discarded axe. He could see Tiffany's eyes, white and staring as her body swayed with the wind that whipped around the corners of the house. Hidden in the shadow, she waited for him. Her monster was still out there, and Marc shook his head. Only one monster at a time, Little Tiffany. He could only stop one monster at a time.

Chapter 25

Shock and disbelief were how Liz would describe it. How could her mother do this? First her father, now her mom? She watched with a jaw too weak and numb from the idea to even mouth a single word as her brother Stevie was wiggled into his big winter coat.

"You'll be OK, hun. I'll only be gone for a short time. Plus, your father said that he would only be away for a little while with Mr. Lawrence," her mom said while she finished stuffing a half foot thick pile of diapers into their carrying bag. "I bet I'll be back before they are and it will be barely past lunch by then."

Liz eyed the digital clock above the stove.

10:59

Her mom better come back quickly if she wanted to return by lunch. Where was she going to go anyway? She hadn't left the house since they moved in a few days ago. She had no friends or family in the area. If she was going to the store, why wouldn't she take her as well?

"But Mom," Liz finally managed to stammer. She side-stepped her way over to the middle of the foyer, her back against the wall and her eyes following the stairwell up toward her room. "I'm not sure I'm old enough to be alone yet."

It was a lie, and she knew it. She had been begging her parents since she was nine to let her stay home alone. She was almost a grown woman, and she didn't need a babysitter.

"I remember when I was your age. I could cook and clean," her mom started in. Liz fought the urge to roll her eyes but failed miserably. "My parents would have left me for days if it weren't illegal, and sometimes they did anyway. I know you'll be OK. I have faith in you."

Liz could feel the back of her throat closing shut, and the inside of her mouth was going dry. What could she say to stop her mom? Mr. Lawrence hadn't looked like he was willing to let her father stay, though she had demanded a reason they both couldn't wait and help put up the tree. Her father, though she could see the disappointment in his eyes, looked like he had no other choice. He left it to their mom to watch over both of them, and now she was leaving as well.

"Are you sure I can't go with you?" Liz managed to say.

Her boots were right by the door, and she was pretty certain that her coat was still warm from when she had taken it off. She could be ready much quicker than her mom could get Stevie seated in his car seat.

"I promise I won't be any problem. You can even leave me in the car while you run inside."

Her mom stopped with a bottle of baby powder held over the bag. Stevie giggled and tossed his pacifier at the opening and watched it bounce away and roll to the edge of the counter and fall.

"And you know where I'm going how?"

Her mom turned toward her, the pacifier either not noticed or not cared about.

"Uh, I don't know. I just figure you're gonna run into the Central Market or something. There really isn't much else to do here, yet. I could sit in the car and finish my book. I promise I'll be quiet."

Cold sweat ran down the back of her neck, tickling the skin underneath her thick ponytail. She could feel the dread welling up in the middle of her chest, the need to look into the shadows that still poured out of the darkened room she hadn't slept in since the other night overpowering. Her father hadn't moved the door outside, though at least it wasn't standing upright anymore. She could see only the very edge of it where it laid on its side, and the white paint stood out against the darkness that filled the hallway above.

"Don't you go on about ghosts and other scary dreams, Liz. I know you were frightened the other night," her mom said before turning back to the open carrier. "You've got a chance to be a big girl now. You don't want Stevie to grow up knowing that his big sister is frightened of ghosts in the shadows do you?"

Liz didn't want that, but she also didn't want him to know what she knew. There was something up there, she had seen it with her own eyes. She could still feel the strength of it pulling the blanket out of her grip. It wanted her; maybe it even wanted Stevie. How could she convince her parents that whatever was in this house was real? Wetness trickled down her cheeks, and she slumped against the wall.

"Mom, you can't leave me here, I'm scared. Take me with you, please."

Her mom sighed before she zipped up her brother's diaper bag. Without answering, she picked him up and hefted him onto her upper arm and he wrapped his arms around her neck.

"Liz, straighten yourself up," she said, looking down into Liz's eyes. "There is nothing to be afraid of. I'll be right back, and you'll barely even notice I'm gone. Get the fire going real warm and curl up with that book of yours. I'll have your father buy you another one for Christmas if you can finish it before I get home, and I don't want to hear another word about you being scared of this house. Do I make myself clear?"

The tears burned at the corner of Liz's eyes. The ball of fear was so heavy in her chest. She could feel the eyes looking down at her already. They were there at the top of the steps, waiting for their chance to snatch her and drag her away.

She couldn't find the nerve to answer, though. Instead, she nodded and shrugged her shoulders. It would only be an hour or two, right? She could do this. Her mom was correct, she was a grown up now.

"Remember, keep yourself warm, and I'll be right back," her

mom said. She turned and opened the door to the front porch. "Stay inside. It's getting pretty cold as it is and I don't want you to accidentally lock yourself out."

Without waiting, her mom shut the door behind her, and Liz could hear her boots go down the steps and leave the house behind. She took a deep breath to steady her pounding nerves. There wasn't going to be much to this. She'd throw two more logs on the fire and read the rest of her book. She had two hundred pages left. That would give her mom two to three hours to get back, or she'd get a new book. Sniffing hard to calm her breathing, she headed into the living room with her head held high. She could do this, right?

Chapter 26

Only seventy-five pages left to go. Liz shut the book, strings of blue and gray hanging out to mark the page while she let it sit on the thick arm of her new favorite chair. She closed her eyes and let her head sink into the thick fabric while the wood logs crackled and warmed her legs. She had put two new pieces into the hot embers when her mother had first left, but now she considered tossing in a third. The warmth was comforting, her legs at their closest almost too warm, but it was better than the cold she could feel at her back.

Opening her eyes, she could see the shadows lengthening in the front yard. The sun had crossed overhead already and was inching its way toward the trees to the west, and it soon would begin to darken into another cold night. Christmas Eve of all nights. Where were her parents? Her father had left with Mr. Lawrence earlier in the morning and hadn't returned. Mom had taken Stevie with her into town. Why? She didn't know and couldn't get it off of her mind. She had tried desperately to beg her mom to take her with her. Why hadn't she been allowed to go? She was twelve and more than old enough to watch herself for a few hours but in this house? She had locked herself to sitting next to the fire, refusing to take more than a quick trip to the bathroom where she left the light on and the door open.

In desperation, she tried to fall into the story of her book, but the puzzle left by her mother wouldn't let her concentrate. She'd probably have to reread this one anyway. It was her favorite series, and she could barely tell where the characters were. The words only blurred in her mind as she wandered off into something else, either about her parents or this house.

It had felt like her first real home since they moved from LA, but now it was different. She could barely fathom the idea of stepping away from her chair. She had all the lights on the first floor up bright. Lit up like the middle of the day; she couldn't see a single shadow in the house. This was until she looked up the stairs. Darkness reigned up there, and it laughed at her feeble attempts to keep it at bay. She tugged at her blanket and pinched it tighter around her shoulders. It was warm here; there was no reason for her to leave this chair until her mom or dad returned.

She was growing thirsty, but she knew she could ignore it. They may say she was a grown up, and in front of the adults she was going to do everything she could to act like one, but here, alone, there was nothing that was going to force her to leave the comfort of this warm fire. There were starving children in Africa who were lucky to ever get a clean glass of water; she could go another hour without iced tea. Nodding her head to reaffirm that very thought to herself, she picked up her book and opened it back up. Another hour or so and her dad would owe her another book. She could do this.

CRASH!

Liz threw her book up into the air and jumped from her chair. Crouched behind the thick arms, she looked toward the foyer and waited for something to come around the corner.

What was that?

She could feel her heart racing once again. Her nerves were tired, and her hands shook as they gripped the chair. There was something in the house, and she knew it. Where was the phone? She could call her dad. Maybe Mr. Lawrence would drive him back from wherever they had gone. She looked around and saw nothing. Small bits of wood and charred bark lay scattered before the stove's screen and her book had landed face down at the far edge of the stone that lined itself along the wall.

SCRATCH!

Liz gasped and held her breath. She sat down on the floor and tried to curl herself as small as she could against the side of the loveseat. That was the same noise she had heard scratching the ceiling above her room. Her mind swam, and she wanted to scream. The temperature in the room was beginning to grow colder, and she could feel the chills running down her back. Whatever it was in her room was going to come down the stairs. She had to run. There was no time left to call her parents.

Her boots and jacket were right near the door. She was fast. She could run and grab them before she made it out the front. She'd make it to the road and start walking back toward town. She knew the way. Dad had made sure she knew where they were going each time they left. She could do this.

Wiping her hands on her legs, she pushed herself off the floor and onto her knees.

Thump!

Heavy boot steps landed on the floor at the top of the stairs. Her knees wobbled and threatened to send her back to the ground, but she bit her lower lip to stop herself from screaming. She was a grown up. She wouldn't scream like she did before. She could make it. It was only a few dozen feet to the front door and out. Taking a deep breath, she turned and crouched behind the chair. It was now or never.

Without warning the lights in the kitchen and foyer blinked out. Darkness and shadow exploded into the rooms, and she could no longer see past the wall that marked the end of the living room.

No light, nothing could break through the thick cloud of shadow. Tears burst from her eyes, but she bit harder on her lip to stop the scream that burned in her chest. Where was she to go? She couldn't run into the darkness; it waited for her in there. She could feel it; she could hear it in her mind as it waited to claim her.

Turning her eyes, she could see the sun outside. The shadows had already grown longer, but there was still light. Maybe she could somehow get through the window and run for it. Anything was better than being taken by whatever it was that wanted her. Digging her nails into the cloth of her chair, she took a deep breath and steadied herself to run.

With a scratch that rang in her ears, the curtains slammed together in front of the glass. Something pulled them together, and Liz backed away from her hiding spot. This couldn't be happening. Burning seared the back of her pants and shirt when she stepped against the fireplace. Screaming from the pain, she tripped to the side and brought the fireplace tools down with her. Tears flowed from her eyes as she pulled herself to the wall. The shadows had entered the living room and were slowly rolling across the wooden floor. There was no life within that darkness. Only death and fear waited for her as it approached. She kicked with her feet but didn't move far, her back flattening against the wall. Her right hand wrapped around a metal handle, the darkness now only a few feet from her.

"What do you want?" she screamed.

She held the metal poker in front of her. Shaking with weakness, the feeble weapon was of little use as even the light from the burning logs flickered now that the shadows had reached her chair. She sobbed uncontrollably and barely held onto the iron weapon. Deep red eyes stared back at her. There was no one to save her. It had finally reached her, and there was nowhere to go.

With a gust of wind as cold as ice, the fire within the family's fireplace smothered out and sent a thin stream of stale smoke high into the sky above the house. Screams of a young girl echoed into the silence of a chilly afternoon, where there wasn't a living soul within miles to hear her.

Chapter 27

"What about these?" Marc asked, the black and white photos spread across the oak table.

White blinding light reflected off the glossy paper and glared across the empty white room. Two cameras blinked red in opposite corners, the videos recording in a closet down the hall. The buzzing of the fan in the vent above did nothing but push warm air and dig deeper into the split that was tearing his mind apart from the inside.

He watched as Robert ran his finger over the photos, as little emotion on his face as there was when he had entered the room. The man remained a stone, answering in only short sentences and never giving Marc a single idea that he was worried or disturbed by the amount of evidence laying in front of him.

"You have nothing to say?" Marc asked again, pulling the chair across from the father out and sitting down.

His lungs burned for another cigarette, but he had smoked the last after arriving, and he swore to God he wasn't going to forget to stop by the Central Market again.

Robert picked his eyes up from the photos, his face calm and his shoulders relaxed. Marc knew he'd have to wait this one out. How long could he go, though? There was that one ten years ago. The street banger had made it twenty-seven hours before he finally spilled it all. He even gave up what he did to his neighbor's dog when he was thirteen years old. Marc had barely made it through that, hanging on by threads and endless coffees until that final moment when the man had started to cry.

"Fourteen murders have your name on them, Robert. Fourteen life sentences. That's a long time to spend behind bars," Marc said, to no reaction. "You won't even get to see your daughter's grandkids at that rate."

Robert's eyes narrowed. Finally, a reaction.

"You do know it will destroy her, don't you? A trial, the press. Do you know what that does to a little girl like her?" Marc began picking up the photos. "Little Liz and her serial killer father. I can see the headlines now."

"Have it all figured out, don't you, Detective Stutton?" Robert asked.

He pushed himself away from the table and crossed his arms over his chest.

"Young girls are resilient, though. Maybe she won't grow up to hate you for what you've done. You seem to have been a good father to her. I could even see her naming a son after you. Of course, she'd have to hide who you really are."

With that statement, Robert smiled. Marc flipped the pencil in between his fingers, though the urge to snap it screamed in the back on his mind.

"I like your resilience, Detective. You did a fine job there, introducing yourself as if you were our new neighbor, welcoming us to the community. I think you even had Amy convinced."

Marc sat there in silence. Only had Amy fooled?

"And you are going to have me believe that you knew all along?" Marc asked with a smile.

Robert chuckled to himself.

"Mrs. Ziegler wanted me to say hi to whomever you were. She's a nice old lady. Been in Portswell all her life. Only Lawrence she knew died some twenty years ago." Robert leaned forward, his elbows resting on the table. "I would say I had my ideas. But, that still brings us to why we are here. What do these pictures have to do with me?"

Overconfident. That was how they always started. Marc rolled up his sleeves, bunching them at his elbows. The room was getting warm, uncomfortably warm, he hoped.

"You leave a pretty large swath of destruction wherever you go, Robert. It really isn't that hard to find."

"I thought you brought me here to talk about this bruise on my face. Didn't you say you had a few questions to ask about the other day?" Robert asked.

Trying to change the subject. This man wasn't as smart as he thought he was. Marc had played this game a hundred times.

"First LA, then Illinois and Maryland. What were your plans here in Portswell, Robert? Kill a couple of farmers or campers gone astray?"

Robert looked down at his watch. It was a nice time piece. Rolex, though it could be a fake.

"Do you have anything to ask me about this bruise or not, Detective? I think I'd like to go home now—I have a tree I promised to put up with Liz, and it's getting late already."

"You'll go when I'm done talking with you, and that's only if you can convince me you had nothing to do with those men in those photos."

A smile inched its way across the father's face. Marc wanted to slap him. Something deep down told him he still didn't have control of this situation. This murderer was playing him, and he knew it. What was he missing? Fourteen dead bodies and he ends up here in the middle of nowhere. A knuckle to the temple didn't relieve the pain as Marc closed his eyes.

"How about I make this easy on you, Detective. Go outside in the hall and get yourself something to drink and take a Tylenol or two. Talk to your boss out there and come back in. If you have any questions relating to this bruise on my face, I'll be right here to talk to you. If not, I think I'll be taking that ride you offered back to my house. We left my Prius in the driveway."

The man winked and reached forward, his fingertips running over the edge of the manila folder before he pushed it closer to where Marc sat.

Anger welled up inside as Marc looked up at the cameras that flashed red, over and over in aggravating cadence. The captain was probably watching. This was his realm, not those doughnut eating, pistol carrying park rangers. He was here to catch monsters like Robert. How could he be letting this one slip away?

With a grunt, Marc pushed himself from the table.

"I do think I need a quick drink. When I come back, I'll be asking you more questions about these," Marc promised, waving the folder in front of Robert's face.

Outside in the hall, the cooler air swirled his mind as he breathed it in. It was warm in that room; he hadn't realized how bad it was until now.

"Detective, can I have a word with you?" The captain asked.

The commanding officer was standing with only one foot in the hallway, the other in the recording closet. So, he had been watching.

Marc wiped away the sweat from his brow and took another deep breath. What words of advice was he going to have to swallow now?

"Pretty rough in there, isn't it?" The captain asked, not looking at Marc as he sat back down on the foldout chair positioned in front of four eight-inch black and white monitors.

Two of them displayed an empty room, while two watched as Robert relaxed in his chair and picked at some dirt from beneath his nails.

"I'll break him. It will take a while, he's a strong one, they always break in the end. I haven't found one who hasn't."

The officer nodded his head without saying anything, his eyes locked to the video screens.

"Did you need anything from me, Captain?"

"Need anything? Oh, no. I do have this for you, though," he answered.

Opening the drawer to the table, he pulled out a folded fax sheet with API printed in the center.

Marc took the offering and opened it up. As the others had been, there wasn't more than a line or two. Short and sweet, his instructions left no room for questions, but a sea worth of options.

End Investigation. All Surveillance to End Immediately.

He had to read over the two sentence message a couple of times. His department was ordering him off the case already? He finally had a reason to bring the man in. It was shaky evidence at best, but if they would give him enough time he knew he could break him.

"Wasn't good news, was it?" the captain asked before he sipped from his Styrofoam coffee cup.

"No, it wasn't."

"It never is when Albany's involved. Gonna have to cut him loose."

Marc squeezed his fists until his knuckles cracked.

"I can still keep him here on the assault charges from the market."

The captain turned, a look of pity on his face.

"About that. I got a call from lock-up. It looks like your boys posted bail. Also sent a message that they recanted their story. They aren't sure who hit them, but they were certain it wasn't your man in there."

Marc's shoulders withered under the pressure of the officer's reassuring grip as he stood to leave the room.

"When did this happen?" Marc asked.

"Not long after you got here. I was told a friend of theirs in some out of town car pulled up and posted bail. I wanted to see what you could get, but now it's obvious we aren't going anywhere," the captain said as he stepped back into the hallway. "Cut him loose and go find those boys. It's Christmas Eve, and I don't want them causing any more trouble until after the holiday."

Pain seared through Marc's head as he leaned against the small room's door frame. Who bailed them out? His only chance to break this case had slipped through his fingers. But why? Throwing the folder down in front of the monitors, he turned and went to release the monster back into the world.

Chapter 28

"Sorry I wasn't able to help you out, Detective," Robert said with his hand extended.

Marc took it in his own and was surprised at how strong his grip had become. Like iron wrapping around each of his fingers, he wasn't sure he was going to get his arm back.

"I wouldn't leave town if I were you. There will be more questions to ask, and I know where you live."

"That you do, Detective. That you do."

Robert turned and followed one of the town deputies to his cruiser parked in the nearly empty lot. Marc pulled his jacket tighter around himself as he watched them go. There was a confidence in the man's walk, and the printed note in Marc's pocket burned like a brand that would scar him for the rest of his life.

He was letting a monster slip through the cracks, and there wasn't anything he could do about it. Why was Albany pulling him from the case? Didn't they realize how dangerous it was to let him roam the street free?

Marc lit the cigarette he had bummed from Missy at the reception desk. It was a menthol. He never liked menthols, but it was better than nothing. Warmth filled his lungs before he blew the white smoke into the air. His head now felt three times larger than his skull, the blood from his heart pounding in his ears, and he could see Tiffany standing in the corner near the entrance to the station with her eyes locked on the same two men he watched get into the car at the end of the row.

Did she know what he was? Maybe she had some sense that those who were still living couldn't feel. No matter what Albany said, he wasn't going to give this up. There were two young kids in that house, and they were in danger the longer that man lived under the same roof. Marc took in the final drag, tossed the butt on the ground, and stuffed it out with his shoe.

First things first. He needed to find out how those two Neanderthals got themselves out and back on the street. No good Samaritan shows up on Christmas Eve and bails two drunks out for $20,000 each. He would get answers from someone today, no matter how much it cost him.

***

Lock-up, as he expected, was empty. A single State Trooper SUV sat out front, the emblem of New York State painted in gold on its blue side, and a small layer of snow sat on the hood and roof.

Marc had barely noticed that it started snowing. He had grown accustomed to six months of spitting snow almost every day that it never even registered in his mind until it began to pile up.

Outside, he could feel the temperature was already a few degrees lower than it was when he had left the precinct. It was going to be a very cold Christmas Eve, and the clouds above his head were darkening from more than the fading sun. If they were lucky it would blow over and the weathermen would be wrong again. The bite of the air on Marc's tongue told him differently. There would be a fresh layer of white over Portswell by the morning, and he probably wouldn't be measuring it in inches.

"So which of you called to let me know our guests had gotten themselves out?" Marc asked the moment his shoes hit the lobby floor.

The woman behind the desk, a different one from before, in her fifties with a bush of red hair on her head, nodded toward the guard at the door. Officer Stewarts opened one eye from where he leaned back in his chair.

"Stewarts, this lovely lady says you're the one who called in when our two esteemed guests found themselves a rich uncle."

The officer dropped his chair forward and stood. He was larger on his feet than he appeared in his chair.

"Not an uncle, I'd say more of a sugar momma."

Marc raised his eyebrow at that.

"Go on."

"She was young, and had looks worth killing for."

"If you say so," the woman behind the desk mumbled before tapping on her phone with the tip of a pressed-on nail.

"Anything else you can describe her with, officer? There are a lot of nice looking women in this world."

"Not like this one. She was gorgeous, even with a face as cold as ice. A smile on a face like that could make someone believe global warming actually existed."

"Officer!" Marc let the anger grumble in his voice.

"Alright, keep your pants on. She was dressed real nice, some real expensive purple coat. Didn't match that orange car of hers, though. You could see her coming from a mile away, stupid city folk and their sissy cars."

"What? What kind of car, did you get the model?"

"It was a Toyota Prius. Plate XQT 753," the woman behind the desk answered.

Stewarts turned and looked at her, anger behind his eyes. Marc didn't care if she stole the man's thunder. This couldn't be a coincidence.

"She bailed both of them out?" Marc asked.

"Yep, paid in a cashier's check. She only wanted the smart one, Tony, but he insisted the other come as well. Said it was a package deal or no deal at all," she answered.

"Never seen jailbirds make demands from someone bailing them out, have you, Detective?"

"No I haven't," Marc said.

He turned on his heels and headed back through the glass front door. White lights danced before his eyes and the pain in his head doubled as the cold bit into his skin. Medicine would have to wait. He had to get back to the house. Maybe he had it all wrong. Maybe he had brought in the wrong monster.

Chapter 29

"Daddy!" Lis screamed.

Every word scratched at the back of her throat. She didn't know how long she had been here; time and space meant nothing in a world of darkness. There was no light. She could rub her hands over her face and still not see anything.

Was she dead?

She didn't think so. She could still feel her arms and legs, and pinching her skin hurt as it always did, but where was she? Weariness had taken everything from her when the demon had overcome her. There had been no pain, but the horror had almost burst her heart. She could still feel it beating against the inside of her chest, thumping its way as it tried to rip from her skin.

Her dad would come and get her. She had to still be in the house, wasn't she? There was no way for her to tell. When she had awoken, her world no longer existed. If she tried to walk, it didn't feel like she moved. Weightless, she remained in the void, waiting for whatever had taken her to finally come back.

"Daddy, where are you?" she whimpered.

Or did she?

She could no longer tell. Her existence was silent, the sound of her thoughts and screams the only thing that reached her ears. She was alone. They would never find her. Who could? They didn't believe the monster even existed. Now she would become one of those missing children you see on the wall at supermarkets.

Have you seen this child?

She could see her face in black and white, smiling and happy. Her face hurt, and her skin felt sticky from the dried tears. What was she to do? Fight back? A little girl against a demon that can black out an entire house. There was no fight left in her; she could feel it down to her bones.

"You have been a naughty girl this year," the voice from the darkness said.

Like an animal, the words were more growl than human.

Liz spun but could see nothing. A heavy weight pressed down on her shoulders, a pressure that gripped her from the inside. The demon was close; it had to be.

"Where am I? What have you done?"

Silence was her only companion. Dread and weight continued to crush her, her knees beginning to weaken beneath the onslaught.

"Children obey their parents, both the father and the mother, and you have brought anything but joy to both."

Tears fell anew from Liz's eyes. What was this thing talking about? It was a monster; how could it know if she made her parents happy?

"Take me back to my mom and dad!"

She fell to her knees, sobs of heartache convulsing in her chest.

"Who says they want you back? Your parents have another child to watch over. Maybe he will turn out better than you and lead a better life."

Cold air washed over Liz's body. It really was over, wasn't it? She sniffed back and tried with what little strength she had to grab onto something she could fight with. Her father would never give up, and she was his daughter. A small flame sparked within her. Taking slow breaths, she worked the embers until she could feel them begin to warm her from the inside.

"I was a good daughter to my parents. I always did what they asked of me. You have to let me go, you monster!"

Overwhelming dread drained the pulsing adrenaline from her blood, and she fell to her rear. She wanted to cry, but a voice in her head refused to let the tears continue.

"If you meant so much to them, then why did they not believe you? Are you so easily pushed aside?" the demon asked.

It was still all around her; she could feel it breathe as the darkness touched and then receded from her skin. The shadows were part of it, and within the void, all of what scared her held her firm.

"My parents have not forgotten me," she said, though out of nowhere the possibility took a small grasp in the back of her mind.

"Then watch and see. Your world is over, and you are now mine. Behold their world without you in it."

Grey smoke swirled at Liz's feet. Small clouds of dust lifted from between her ankles, congealing until it formed an opening just outside her reach.

"Watch your parents. See what you have done."

Liz could see her mom pacing in the kitchen with Stevie on her shoulder. The mist in front of her was like looking through a window suspended in the air; her mom was so close she could almost reach out and touch her.

"Are you sure this will work?" her mom asked.

Stevie hugged one arm around her neck as she walked the length of the kitchen. His pacifier bobbed back and forth in his mouth, and his blue footie pajama's kicked against his mother's chest while his eyes stared out beyond the mirror's reach.

"How hard can it be? He's your husband, and you didn't even want to get Carl out," a male voice Liz recognized said. "Don't you worry your pretty little head off. We've got this covered, though you may owe both of us a little extra when this night is through."

A look of disgust snapped across her mother's face, then a smile as wicked as Liz could ever imagine warmed across her features.

"I'm going to guess he'll be here soon. If you see my daughter, be careful to leave her out of it," her mom said before she placed Stevie on the counter. "I won't exactly hold it against you, but try to keep things clean."

Her little brother squealed and blew bubbles with his hands up in the air. He never did like being put down.

Liz's throat was as dry as the desert. What was her mom talking about? Who were these men inside her house? Why wasn't her father there? Questions ran without answers through her head as she tried to get closer. Like watching the TV, the fear of the demon that held her captive was temporarily forgotten.

"I think he's here, boss," a second male voice said.

"Quick you fools, hide!" her mother ordered.

Her mother scooped up her brother and bolted out of the kitchen. The magical opening followed as she raced across the foyer and turned up the stairs. Shadows and darkness hid the second floor, and Liz's eyes locked on the broken door that still rested against the wall to her room.

"Liz, Amy, I'm home!" her father called out before he shut the door.

Liz could feel the vibrations as it slammed against its frame beneath her feet. She looked away from her father and into the darkness. She couldn't see the monster, but the presence still weighed itself against her. It couldn't be that far away.

"Ssh! What are you thinking?" her mom said in a whisper that was only slightly lower than a shout.

Slowly, she pulled her bedroom door shut and turned down the stairs.

"Stevie finally laid down. Do you want to wake him up?" her mom said, a scowl on her face.

"Where is Liz? I didn't mean to be gone this long," her father said. "Darn Lawrence, that man has some crazy stories."

Her mom waved a hand over her shoulder and headed toward the kitchen without a word. Liz watched as her father took off his jacket and hung it up, with a quick glance into the living room. She guessed he was still looking for her.

"Isn't she with you?" her mom asked.

She leaned against the kitchen table and took a long, hard swallow of what remained of her wine glass.

"No, I left with Lawrence hours ago. Are you telling me you don't know where she is?"

Her father's eyes narrowed as he entered the kitchen. His shoulders rolled forward, and his hands balled when her mother shrugged her shoulders.

"She was with you when you dragged that damn tree over here. Then you left with our neighbor. I thought she went with you."

A wet smack echoed across the lower floor of the house as Liz watched her father's face slam to the side.

"Looks like the faithful old man has finally come home," one of the men said.

He smiled from ear to ear as he watched her father hold onto his jaw, a hard look in his eyes she had never seen before.

"Tony, don't let him have a chance!" her mom shouted.

Liz's heart jumped. That was Tony!

A second slap rang out before a thud shook the floor at her feet when her father hit the ground. A second man stepped out from the shadows with a piece of firewood in his hand.

Her father struggled to get to his feet, a bloody hand smearing itself against the wall as he tried to push himself up.

"Shut up, Amy. Carl and I owe this one a good time tonight. He put two of our brothers into the hospital," Tony said. He lowered his face down to where he was only inches away from her father's bloody chin. "We are going to have fun tonight, old man."

Blood sprayed across the floor, and Tony screamed as he fell backward. Liz could see where his nose bent sharply to the side and dark fluid poured out like a faucet. Her father sprang to his feet, but before he could turn, the block in Carl's hand slammed into his stomach. Liz squeezed her midsection as she tried to scream out to help him. The first blow toppled her father to the ground; the second rocked his head back, and he left a fist-sized hole in the wall behind him. Rolling to the floor, he didn't move when Tony stopped swearing and kicked him in the chest.

Liz lost control of her tears, and the magical opening began to fade. She could see her mother shouting, her lips and arms moving wildly, but no words reached where Liz remained trapped. She wanted to throw up. Her stomach lurched as the sight of the weapon smashing into her father's bloody face replayed over and over in her mind.

The demon was next to her again. It's presence was no comparison to the anguish she felt with what was happening to her family.

"It looks like you aren't the only one who has been bad this year," the demon said.

Liz turned. She could see it now. Its red eyes burned with satisfaction. It had her; it had them all if it wanted to. Her father's strength exploded in her when she felt it draw closer. He was a fighter, and so was she. He would continue to fight those men, he would not give up, because if he did he would never be able to help her or Stevie.

She would fight too. She would not give up.

"Are you going to let this happen? I thought you took all of those who were bad on Christmas Eve, or do you only take children?"

The shadows felt like ice. Her skin prickled as she challenged it.

"My father isn't scared of you. Those men down there aren't scared of you. I am not scared of you!"

The eyes disappeared. Shivers ran down her spine as the temperature continued to drop.

"Tonight, we will see who deserves to see the light again," the demon said.

Liz spun on her heals. She could hear the hissing and the demon's steps all around her. What had she done? She covered her mouth with her hands. What had she done?

Chapter 30

Silence.

She was alone. The trembling of her fingers had stopped, but the worrying of her mind raced faster than a rumor spread around school.

The demon had vanished. Darkness still surrounded her. She floated in a void, weightless and without substance, but the evil no longer touched her skin. What was it going to do? She wished she could see through the opening again, if only to see if her father was OK. He looked lifeless when he fell to the floor. What had her mother done?

Liz sobbed for what felt like the thousandth time. No tears would fall, her eyes burned dry from the salt and the fear. Soft and smooth, she felt the thick cloud around her begin to circulate. Small shades of gray began to lighten the black as the rolling substance collected at her feet.

The magic was returning. She pushed herself to her knees and waited as it built in strength. She was going to see what was going on. Maybe she could reach out to them. The monster was gone; it wouldn't be able to stop her.

Slow and steady, the smoke opened up before her. She could see inside the kitchen. Her mother sat at the table, another glass of wine shaking in her hand as Tony lit a cigarette that sat between her lips. Blood, red and smeared, stretched from where her father had fallen, out to where she couldn't see it any longer.

Liz squeezed her hands when she felt them begin to shake. There was a lot of blood, too much for one person to bleed. Where was he, and where was that one named Carl?

“What are we going to do with him now?” her mom asked.

She swallowed the entire glass in one chug. Tony smiled from behind a cloth soaked red and pressed against his nose.

“Calm down, girl. He isn’t gonna hurt you anymore,” he said. He pulled the rag away and fresh blood leaked out. “Asshole did a number to my face. Gonna make him pay for that. Carl is already getting the car ready.”

“What about Liz?” her mom asked, an unsteady hand toppling over an empty wine bottle.

“Your daughter?”

The eyebrows on her mom’s face lifted, but she didn’t say a word.

“You can do what you want with her. Lie to her, get rid of her. Little kids weren’t part of the deal. I have my limits, even for a nice piece of ass like you.”

Her mom swung out an open hand at the man’s face. He caught it long before her slow reactions could reach him.

“Now, now. Don’t get all sentimental on me.”

Liz watched as he pulled her close and shoved his lips against her. Blood ran down the side of her cheek and dripped from her chin before she pushed him away.

“Remember our deal,” Tony said.

He stood up and tossed the rag across the table.

“Liz, I’m sorry,” her father’s voice called out from the darkness.

The gray window evaporated in an instant as Liz fell backward.

“Dad?” she asked.

“Liz, is that you?”

His voice was weak, and she could hear him cough twice between words.

“Dad, where are you?”

“I think I’m in the basement. It’s rather dark down here. Where are you?”

She looked around. The darkness was too deep for her to see. Could she be in the basement as well?

“The demon took me, Dad,” she said. “There is so much

darkness here. I can't see you, but maybe I'm close."

Liz began to shuffle around on her hands and knees. Her father had to be close. How could she hear him otherwise?

"What do you mean the demon took you? This isn't a time for stories, Liz."

She stopped where she was. There was anger in his voice, but how could she make him believe?

"It came for me when mom left with Stevie. The shadows darkened everything. It's big, Dad, and I'm scared."

"What do you mean your mom left you when she took Stevie?" her father asked, his voice angry and stronger than it was before.

Liz felt the air around her begin to warm. She looked around, watching for the fire-red eyes to come back and the monster to find out what she was doing.

"Liz?"

"Yeah, right after you and Mr. Lawrence took off this morning, she said she had to run into town. I begged her to let me go, Dad. I swear I did. She told me I was old enough to watch myself," Liz answered. She struggled to keep her tongue from wavering with the emotion. "I tried to get away. I wanted to be strong like you, but it took everything from me. I was so scared."

"Ssh, it's OK, honey. I need to tell you something."

Liz took a deep breath and waited. Silence hung in the air like her only companion, its embrace complete and her father no longer there.

"I've done a lot of bad things in my life. Some things I regret, and some that I will have to answer for one day. Everything changed for me the day you were born. I tried to leave it all behind, take you and your mother somewhere we could be a family, but I've failed."

"No, you haven't!" Liz slid to her knees. "Dad, you've always been there for us. Everything will be OK. You can find me. We'll get Stevie and mom away from those guys. Leave this house and find somewhere new."

He didn't answer. She was alone again. Her ears begged for a response.

"I'm sorry, Liz. There is no other way. If there are other monsters in this house, then they are as lost as I am. I will find you, and I will get you out. Please forgive me if you can, maybe the detective was right."

The burning returned to Liz's eyes as fresh tears dripped down her cheek. What was he going to do? The gray mist swirled around her legs and wrapped itself around her. She could feel tiny hands touching her, feeling her skin and pulling at the edges of her sleeves and ankles.

Opening inches from her face, she could see the basement door locked behind a chair leaned against the handle to keep it shut. Blood pooled at its base and then smeared where it ran below the frame.

Her father was in the basement, but where was she? She could hear footsteps approaching, heavy like boots. A man dressed in a long, dark coat stepped in front of the door. A light dusting of snow covered his shoulders, and he held a dented metal pipe in his hand.

He was going down after her father. She tried to scream, but the words faded before they left her mouth. Bright red eyes appeared behind the man's shoulder. Shadows as dark as night pooled in the corner of the small entry way to the downstairs bathroom. The demon was there, and its eyes burned with fury.

Chapter 31

Heavy snow fell across Portswell as Marc tore down Main Street in his Malibu. Its engine rattled like a tin can with a stone inside, and his heater sputtered as it blew in warm air with bursts of a chilly breeze that continued to drop in temperature. Giant white flakes, falling like rain, swerved in the air, pressing into his windshield and threatening to mesmerize his eyes if he looked into them too long.

Backup was at least thirty minutes away. He had called for aid the moment he left lock-up, but there was no one still in town. Those who remained scattered themselves to distant roads, probably asleep and hoping for a quiet holiday.

That wouldn't be the case tonight. Marc turned his windshield wipers up to max speed as he approached the sharp bend where the road turned away from the lake. The tiny motors that pumped with the blades cried over the noise of the engine, almost every part of his car needing a repair, or simply junked with other have been vehicles left to rot into history.

They had a two hour lead on him, and the deputy would have dropped Robert off already. Everything was going to be a mess, a real bloody mess.

How could he have missed this? Was he that naive? Robert wasn't the monster; he wasn't the one leaving the wake of death in their trail. He was a father trying to keep his family safe. Marc could still see her cold eyes staring at him the day he first introduced himself. She was strong and calculated. If anyone got in her way, she would stomp them out like a bug. Tonight, it looked like she had set her gaze on her family. Would it stop at the father? Marc hoped so. He couldn't fathom the idea of another young, innocent child dying on his watch. Not in this town, not in that house.

Against his will, his eyes lifted from the road ahead, the blinding snow building in intensity. She was behind him. Little Tiffany and her dead eyes, dark and as deep as the worst pits of hell. He could smell the putrid waste, thick and earthy, as she sat in the backseat and waited. She was returning home. Would she welcome the newest victims? Take their small hands into hers and lead them into an afterlife of memories and dreams that never happened?

Blood dripped from the girl's hairline. Black and thick, it oozed its way between her eyes and dripped from the tip of her nose. Marc shook his head; he could feel the sweat beading just above his eyebrows. Wiping it away with the back of his hand, he took a glance to make sure his scalp wasn't bleeding. It wasn't. The back of his sleeve was wet but clear.

Rrrrr

The engine roared and the RPMs soared as the back tires lost traction and Marc squeezed the wheel. The back end of the Malibu swung to the right, the sheet of snow spiraling in front of his window as he tried desperately to right the car. He could see an overhead light, its yellow glare haloed and fuzzy in the storm, the silver of its aluminum pole speeding directly toward the passenger side. He slammed his foot on the breaks and wrenched his wheel to the right. He felt his stomach roll as the backend overcompensated and spun him in the opposite direction.

He couldn't afford this. He had to make it in time. Releasing the brakes, he turned with everything he had, the steering wheel and his body, but it was too late. The car turned itself entirely around, heading down the road in reverse.

Slam!

Marc's head dented the wheel as his car collided with the piled snow along the road. He could feel himself leaning to the right. Looking, the snow now reached halfway up the passenger side window, and the engine chugged along as it struggled to continue. He wiped his forehead with the back of his hand again, the pain in his skull twice what it ever had been before. Warm and sticky, blood smeared crimson against the white cuffs of his shirt that reached out behind his coat sleeves.

"Damn," he swore to himself.

Turning the wheel back to the road, he could feel it had become loose, but the tires crunched in the snow in return to his commands. Slowly pressing his foot on the gas, the engine revved in response, giving him hopes that the accident hadn't handicapped the vehicle. The car rocked forward an inch or two but quickly slid back as the tires squealed and spun.

Marc slammed his hand into the wheel and felt it give slightly under his hand. He pressed a knuckle into his temple to ease the pain and tried driving away again. Smoke, thin and white, climbed into the sky as the Malibu refused to pull itself from the snowbank. He was stuck, and if he didn't reach the house soon, he knew he was going to be too late.

"Damnit!"

He looked to the back seat as he stepped out. She stared back at him, her pale skin and untiring eyes relentless in his torment. She would never let him go, not until it was over. One day he would join her in the grave. How many would go before him?

With a jolt, the rear driver side door opened, and she vanished. White, blinding heat seared through his mind, but he shook it off. Ripping away the cushion, he punched the code into the lockbox under the bench seating. One shotgun and twelve shells. He had no idea what he was going to be walking into. If he were lucky, he'd be nothing but over-prepared for an uneventful meeting. He doubted it, though. Looking up at the sky above, the snow tickled his skin as it melted on his face. This was going to be a storm this town never forgot. Loading his weapon and stuffing the last few rounds into his pocket, he said a little prayer to a God he knew was as far away as he ever had been and began the long, cold trek to Little Tiffany's house.

Chapter 32

House 996. He had been closer than he thought. Maybe there actually was a God who was doing something to right the wrongs that had been afflicted on so many. Marc crouched as he jogged up the darkened drive. He could see lights flickering down the path, illuminating the white expanse of snow that wrapped the small hamlet within the forest.

He had been a ten-minute jog away from his destination, the dented mailbox a landmark sticking out in defiance of the piles of snow and gravel pushed up by weeks of plows. Having staked out the home for years, he thought he knew its location like the back of his hand, but the storm was changing everything. The world had become a cold and deadly place. The blowing snow and the howl of the wind a reminder that he was not the only one left.

Marc squeezed his numb hands around the barrel and stock of the shotgun, a weapon he hadn't felt beneath the pads of his fingers in years. Filled with doubt of his ability to use the weapon, he pushed away the pain that throbbed between his temples as he marched through the snow. He couldn't afford to lose his senses now, not this close. Stepping out from beneath the tree cover, he could see the house before him. High pointed peaks stood testament against the weather that raged against it, piles of snow growing across its roofs and building against its unmovable walls. Lights burned inside, but only on one side. The upstairs was as dark as the forest behind it, the windows blacked out and lifeless, while downstairs in the foyer and kitchen it raged with a glaring yellow light.

Parked in the drive sat the Prius, the blue truck that dwarfed the car, and a third SUV he didn't recognize. The lights of the SUV were on, and a small column of steam rose from its tailpipe. The car was being warmed up, beads of water dripping down the windows where the cold weather fought its unending battle with the heat. They were already looking to leave. Was he too late?

With a glance at his weapon, Marc made sure it was ready with a click of the safety. He wasn't going to let them get away, not until he made sure the little ones were safe. If he could delay those responsible for all this long enough, his backup would have enough time to arrive. He wouldn't fail this time.

Shadows and the snow disguised his approach. The crunching of snow beneath his frozen loafers was barely audible above the idling engine. A single male bobbed his head, clueless to Marc's approach. Fog had built up inside the windows, and the bass of the speakers rattled the doors like a child's toy while it sat collecting snow on its roof faster than it could melt it.

Marc pressed himself against the back of the truck. Icy fingers ran down his back as the cold penetrated his jacket. He flexed the joints of his right hand. They were stiff but still usable. Taking a steady breath, he crouched and approached the driver from the rear.

A single man, early twenties, sat inside. A can of Molson, open and waiting, remained in the cup-holder as he took a drag of a rolled blunt, the sweet yet skunky smell of marijuana leaking its way out of a tiny crack in the vehicle's window. Marc reached for the handle and squeezed his hand around the cold metal. He could feel his skin sticking, his sweat freezing on contact.

His heart pounded as he counted to two in his head. The man inside still oblivious to his presence, his head still bobbing to the music that pounded with the throbbing of Marc's mind.

"What the?" the kid said before the butt of Marc's rifle slammed into his temple.

He was young, but it didn't matter. He knew why he was here; he knew what his friends were doing. Plus, he was already breaking several laws. Marc felt very little sympathy for him as he cuffed the man's hands behind his head and through the head rest. A large welt was rising to the left of man's eye as his head bobbed freely around his shoulders and he knew the kid would be regretting his life when he woke up. He'd still be alive, though, that was all that mattered.

Marc shut the door quietly and looked up at the house. Maybe he had made it in time for the others.

Boom! Boom!

"Ah!" a woman's voice screamed into the night.

Two more gunshots rang out as flashes lit up the darkness in the living room windows. The heartbeat in Marc's chest froze like the lifeless toes of his feet as he stood in front of the parked cars. He had taken too long; they were already gone. Hesitation, doubt and fear melted away as he charged forward. Fatigue and pain no longer mattered. He was going to get inside. If they had hurt that little girl, they were going to pay. For Tiffany, the one he had failed and who waited for him in every shadow, this would all end tonight.

More shots rang out into the night as he climbed the porch in two bounds. The glass door opened with a slight screech, and the "Merry Christmas" that hung across the top window swayed as he pressed his shoulder against the blue frame and he felt for resistance with the doorknob. It had been locked from inside. Another shot rang out. The wood a foot over his head splintered as the bullet tore through the door.

"Damnit!" Marc yelled.

There was no time to waste. He stepped to the side, leveled his shotgun and pulled the trigger. The first shell exploded against the wood and left a hole the size of his fist where the doorknob had been. Pain throbbed deeply into his chest, his old bones not ready for the shock. Hitting the door with his other shoulder, he felt resistance as the chain lock fought back but quickly gave way. Metal links fell to the floor at his feet, jingling like dropped coins, and the foyer opened up before him, its light blinding and searing as he tried to find a target.

Dark silhouettes danced in the golden light. Marc tried to reason with what he saw. His eyes were burning, but he had little time to choose.

"Freeze, police!" he shouted.

The darkened figure froze in the doorway to the kitchen. A woman's voice continued to scream, piercing his eardrums as the sound threatened to shatter the glass behind him. It was a man, pistol in hand. The shadow stopped, frozen in indecision.

"Put the gun down!" Marc ordered.

Whoever it was looked at Marc then turned his head to the side and raised his pistol again. Hesitation stayed Marc's finger, fear and doubt crippling his judgment as the weapon fired into the open area behind the wall. He could feel his heart frozen in his chest. He couldn't do it. He had never taken a life in the line of duty, the weight of the rifle and responsibility too heavy for a split second before all the strength of his body drained away.

A figure, over seven feet tall, charged into the one who held the pistol. Marc backpedaled until his back pressed itself against the wall, tears running down his cheeks. The second shadow reared back an arm with blades almost a foot long before punching them through the man's chest. Marc's throat dried as colors and shadows began to clear.

Tony, or the man he had known as Tony, stood against the kitchen wall, a pistol dropped down to the floor at his feet. In front of him stood something that Marc could not understand. All muscle, the monster wore tattered rags for clothes that barely clung to darkened skin stretched with every movement. Roughly man like, he could see two horns, curled back and pointed like a bull, extending from its head, where just beneath a heavy set of black eyebrows, two eyes burned red with the fury of hell itself.

Words bubbled out of Tony's mouth, lost in a flood of blood that poured from between his lips. Marc lifted his weapon at the creature who had impaled the man, but his fingers were useless. With the ease of a backhand used to swat a fly, the demon tore out Tony's throat and sent blood in an arc across the wall and into the foyer. A woman's screams echoed through the house as the young man's body fell lifeless to the floor, his innards pooling beneath his rapidly cooling body.

Lost in the chaos and fear, Marc never knew when he pulled the trigger, but the explosion that rocked his body shocked him back into reality. He could feel the vibrations running through his hands and arms, the monster in front of him jolting a step when the shell slammed into its flesh. Turning toward him, he could feel a coldness drain through his veins as the flames set their gaze upon his soul. It was bigger than he imagined, and now that he had become its enemy, he swore it was growing taller. Pumping the shotgun, Marc struggled to keep the weapon in his hands. The vision of Tony's throat slicing open forced its way into his mind and would not leave.

"You can't have her!" a male voice shouted.

A second man charged out from behind the kitchen wall to the left and slammed himself into the side of the demon. Marc in a spot of panic slipped and fell to the ground, his rifle discharging into the roof above the kitchen doorway as he watched the figure tumble against the wall, his weight and that of the demon cracking the drywall on impact. Ceiling dust rained to the floor as the two combatants pushed away. Marc tried to pull himself up as he watched the demon throw the small man into the kitchen, the second's agility beyond compare as he landed on his fcct and skidded to a stop.

It was Robert.

Marc could see blood running from the father's face where it dripped from several cuts and his clothes were soaked red. A knife the size of his forearm materialized in his hand as he began to circle around, the devil's eyes locked on him. With a step and a stab, faster than humanly possible, Marc watched the blade slice through the demon's skin and tear out the side just below the ribs, black blood spraying as a howl shook the house to its core.

"Get the kids!" Robert shouted.

The father dodged as the monster swung at him. He was fast, something on the likes of inhuman, but the monster was something else. Missing with its initial attack, Marc watched as the creature's backhand caught the father across the shoulder and it sent him spiraling in the air until he hit the refrigerator. Rolling away, he barely avoided a weight that would have crushed him as the demon grabbed the fridge and tipped it over like a stack of empty boxes.

"Go, now!" Robert said.

Marc had reached his feet. He didn't know if the man was talking to him or someone else, but he had to give it a try. The last image he saw before he plunged into the darkness of the second floor was of Robert, blade in hand, leaping over the fallen appliance with the weapon aimed directly at the monster's heart.

Chapter 33

He had been here before. Darkness swirled around his body as Marc reached the top step of the stairs. There was no light, the blackness unnatural as he felt his way blindly with an open hand. There would be a door to his left. He knew this house, he had studied its layout for years, but something here was not correct. It felt like several dozen feet had passed, but finally, his fingers grabbed hold as his hand felt the solid purchase of a wooden doorframe.

"Please tell me you are in here," he whispered to himself.

Small white sparkles flickered in front of his vision, but he knew they were only in his head. No sound raged from the floor below him. How could that be? Had Robert been killed? There was no way for him to know. The man could fight, it was obvious, and he knew he would give everything, including his life, to make sure his two children made it out safely, but against what odds? That thing in the kitchen was not from this world. Little Liz had been correct. There was a monster in this house, and it didn't kill for greed or travel its way across this country. It was made to kill for fun. Marc could feel its hunger at only the memory of how it looked, how easily it had torn the life out of a man and left him spilled on the floor.

Marc could feel it all the way up here. It was part of this darkness, its hunger as thick as the void that swirled around his feet and his hands. He had to get the children out. Once outside, he'd make for the highway. The others would be here soon. Surely that would be enough to stop it. One shotgun had barely harmed it, but several would slow it down, at least enough to get the kids away. He would think of what to do after that when it was all finished.

Running his fingers over the wood paneling, he slid his feet forward until he found the round knob that held the door shut. Turning it slowly, he felt a cool breeze of air spill onto his face with the soft sound of a night time lullaby. Stars lit up the ceiling as he stepped in. A baby's pen sat beneath a nightlight of Santa pulling his reindeer where the gentle melody played.

Marc glided his feet over the wooden floor until he could look down onto the tiny mattress. Stevie, curled up around a blanket he held like a teddy bear, slept peacefully with a smile on his face. How could this be? His shotgun alone would have been heard for close to a mile. Here, this child slept as if nothing had happened.

Darkness and ice crept up his spine as Marc turned back to the door. By whatever miracle it was that kept the evil out of this room, he couldn't chance it any longer. There was a monster only a few dozen feet below, and no matter how magical it felt up here, this child was not safe. Marc rested his shotgun against the end of the playpen and pressed his chest against the railing, hoping he could keep Stevie asleep for as long as possible.

Pain bit into Marc's mind with such ferocity that he stumbled and fell to one knee. Jostled, Stevie moaned softly before he pulled the blanket tighter and turned over onto his other side. Nausea turned in Marc's stomach as he rolled onto both knees and looked at the door. Little Tiffany stood in front of the darkness, her deathly white skin a brightness against the evil that rolled behind her.

She would not speak to him, her words only for those who could still reach her, but she said enough as she shook her head slowly from left to right. He wasn't there to take Stevie, but why? Was she protecting him? But how?

Her image faded as the darkness began to push its way into the room. The torture of his mind lessened, and he could feel the churning of his stomach weaken, so he pushed himself to his feet. Reaching for his weapon, he'd leave the little boy there. He didn't understand it, nor did he trust it, but he felt as if Stevie was in good hands. He'd come back for the boy, right after he found his sister. No ghost or demon was going to stop him now. Gripping his shotgun with a renewed strength, Marc shut the door slowly behind him and stepped back into the shadows.

Chapter 34

Fear trickled down Liz's skin like beads of sweat as she sat in total darkness. The gray shadows, the magic that showed her what happened within her home and the power the demon held had vanished. She had watched the beast slice through the man who had opened the cellar door, determined to hurt her father until his own life was torn through a hole in his back. Nausea wretched in her stomach, the taste of vomit lingering in the back of her throat at the gore and the site of the man's innards as they dripped from the monster's claws.

Then it had turned its gaze on the second intruder, the one who had kissed her mother and talked about the plans they had to rid themselves of her dad and herself. He had put up a fight, she could still feel the vibrations all around her as the shots rang out in the darkness. Bullets didn't hurt the demon—they struck, and it bled, but it did not stop. With a single swipe of its hand, the monster had ended another life as easy as it could rip through a wet paper bag.

Nothing could stop it, and her heart was heavy with the dread that told her it was not over. When her father appeared, tattered and bloody at the entrance to the cellar, she had screamed until her lungs ached and when nothing else would come out she begged for him to run. He did not. He attacked the thing instead. Her father, tall and strong, was dwarfed by the creature and he threw himself at it like a dog protecting its master.

At first, she had been in tears. If guns couldn't hurt it, what could he do? Then she watched as wound after wound was inflicted, her father tearing at the very darkness that lived within the monster's soul. It would all be for not; she could still feel the sobs aching in her chest. The demon was too big. The last thing she had seen was her dad flying across the kitchen and landing on the counter, plates and silverware shattered or scattered across the floor. The knife he had fought with, the same one they always cut the Christmas turkey with, its white bone handle and edge that curved to a needle point, had skidded across the tile floor and under the table where her mother cowered in fear.

She tried to hate the woman. The one she had grown to love and admire in every way possible was at fault for all of this. How could she have done this? She had planned for both of them to disappear, but why? She wanted to hate, but the hollow emptiness inside of her could only be filled with pain. The last thing she had seen was the monster, bleeding black bile from several cuts and stab wounds, towering over her father as he struggled to right himself, blood soaking the granite counter where he laid partially inside the kitchen sink.

They could not hear her screams or her begging for mercy. Whatever magic was used to give her the sight had spared her in the end. Retreating back into the darkness, the gray mist evaporated before she could see what had happened with her dad's final moments. Maybe he had died quickly, fighting until the last possible moment to save her and her brother. The thought didn't help, she was lost, and inside only the endless void of despair filled her. Eventually, the creature, Krampus, would come for her. The devil made real, she would be its next victim. Could she fight? Would she? Her hands trembled at the thought. What would a little girl like her be able to do against something like that?

Darkness surrounded her, and without a single ray of light, she was as good as being dead already. What did it matter anymore? She could feel a bead of a tear dangling from the tip of her nose. This wasn't supposed to happen to her. This wasn't supposed to happen to anyone. Where was Santa? Where was God? She squeezed her eyes and felt a fresh stream run down her cheeks. She wiped away the wetness with the back of her hand.

"Always use a tissue, or the edge of your hand if you are going to wipe your nose. A lady never uses her sleeves. The tissue can be thrown away, or your hands can be washed," her mother had always told her. "Unless you are going to go change your shirt every time your nose runs, a lady never uses the blouse that she presents to the world."

Liz chuckled at the thought. What little use that advice had been. The same person who had demanded that she grow up so quickly had planned to discard her like a toy that Stevie no longer played with. What had happened to her family? Why had they come here? Her shoulders ached as the sobs wrenched her body.

"Please make it end," she said to herself. Her voice scratched at the back of her throat, and she could barely hear the words with her own ears. "Just make it stop, please!"

Warm air washed through the darkness as Liz tumbled to her side. She wrapped her arms around her shoulders as she shivered with a cold that sank down deep to her bones. Her eyes burned with dryness as the heated air washed over her body a second time. Something was changing in the shadows, something was coming.

It had returned. She could feel the dread sink in her stomach, but she no longer cared. Let it take her. If it was back, then the rest of her family was dead, and she didn't want to live either. The devil could take her, but it wouldn't have the satisfaction of watching her wailing in fear.

"Liz? Are you up here?" a voice asked through the void.

Light!

She rolled onto her knees and rubbed at her eyes. Faint and gray, she could see the light deep within the shadows.

"I'm here!" she shouted, but the iron taste of blood filled her throat, and she could no longer hear if any words had escaped her lips.

"Liz! Tell me you are up here, child!"

It wasn't her father, but another man. His voice was older, and there was a deep worry behind it. She tried to crawl forward, but there was no way to tell if she was moving. The light remained nothing but a tiny pin prick in a wall of black that grew no larger.

"I'm up here! Please help!"

"I can hear you!" the man shouted, and the light began to grow.

At first, the tiny dot of white struggled to push back the shadows, but with a pulsing strength, she could see the evil recede. The ice-cold grip of fear began to warm itself as she felt it drain from her body. She would be saved. Maybe there was still a chance for them all to get out of this house.

"Hurry! I think he is coming back!" she said, the light growing bright enough that she could see it was the dropped door of the attic.

She was in the attic! Joy and horror flooded through her at the thought. How could she have been so close, yet felt so far away? The room she was in was only slightly larger than her own bedroom, but the entrance looked far enough away she would have to run if she tried to reach it. A heavy weight pushed down on her shoulders as the first hand reached up through the door.

"I'm almost there, sweetie. Your dad sent me to get you," the man said.

Graying hair, thinning at the top, popped over the edge of the attic door. It was Lawrence!

Why was he here?

She didn't care. A smile struggled to lift her lips as the weight of the demon's magic pressed her to the floor. It had returned. She couldn't see it, but its presence was like a second skin. It wanted her, and it wasn't going to let her go.

"Wait, Lawrence!" she screamed.

Her neighbor hesitated as her words reached him. She could see his eyes scanning the room, wide and scared as she was, but his lips were flat and his face determined. Sliding his feet forward, he still couldn't see her, but he held something tucked under his left arm as he felt forward with his right. With each step, he drew closer, and the pressure that held her down worsened to where she could hear the bones of her joints crack.

Pain pulsed through her back and refused to let her lift her head any longer. She could feel the claws scratching her skin, its grip ready to tear into her and feast on her soul, but she could also feel Lawrence's footsteps vibrate the boards beneath her. She had to warn him. She had to try something.

"He's here," her words struggled to cross her lips.

"I know, honey, but so am I," the man said.

His words were suddenly only inches from her face. The pain released from her back as his warm hands glided across the skin of her cheek.

"Your OK. Let's get you and your brother out of here."

The magic that held her in place was gone. The light from the dropped door flooded into the room, and she could see the walls for the first time. Bare, they were nothing but studs and insulation, pink and wrinkled as the roof peaked above her head. Unused wood lay flat on the ground near the wall's edge, covered in dust. She was no more than ten feet from the entrance, yet only a moment ago it had felt like a whole world had separated her from freedom.

"My dad, is he OK?"

"Ssh, we'll check on him after we get you out of here," he whispered as he placed a hand under her arm and started to lift her off the ground. "Can you walk?"

She wanted to scream, but her throat closed, and she could no longer breathe. Her eyes widened as the devil towered over her neighbor. She couldn't stop him. Its eyes burned so brightly she could feel the heat on her skin. She wanted to point, warn the man who was there to save her, but all her strength was gone. Darkness reared up behind him, a hand with claws, black as night and as sharp as blades lifted for a strike that would tear her only hope away.

BOOM!

The rifle under Lawrence's arm exploded and tore into the monster. Shadows splattered in all directions, and the light threw them against the walls.

"We have to get out of here, now!" Lawrence commanded.

With a grunt, he lifted her to her feet. Her knees wobbled and a thousand tiny needles pricked at her feet, but she closed her mind to the pain and leaned against her savior. He swept the room in front of them with his weapon as they inched forward. The demon wasn't gone, there was no body and no blood as there had been in the kitchen.

"He's still here, I can feel him," she whispered.

Evil reached out for her. She could feel its tiny hands scratching at her skin, the need to pull her back stronger with every step they took toward the ladder that would get them out of the attic.

"Almost there, Liz. Just keep moving forward," Lawrence said. "Only a few more feet."

Dark clouds swirled in front of the opening that was now three steps away. She couldn't see the hallway below, the light too bright, but she could see the ladder.

"Jump down, now!" he commanded as he pushed her toward the opening.

Spinning on his heels, he faced the evil that rolled toward them. She could feel the demon everywhere. Her legs felt weak as she took another step away. She would never make it. Even if she climbed down it would get her.

Only two more steps.

"Ah!" she screamed.

Black magic wrapped itself around her legs and bit into the skin as it squeezed tight. With a yank, she tumbled forward.

"She will not leave," the demon's voice called out.

Like thunder at night, the words shook the planks of wood above them and dust mixed with pink fibers began to float down slowly through the air.

"Face me!" Lawrence challenged with a pump of his weapon. "Leave the girl alone and fight someone your own size."

Silence was their only answer. Liz bit down on her lip as the magic gripped tighter into the flesh of her leg. She could feel the blood start to soak the inside of her jeans and the burning that pulsed beneath her skin.

"Help!" she screamed at last.

Lawrence turned toward her. The darkness had formed a loop around her legs, and he looked down to where she lay prone on the ground. He stepped closer to her, his eyes moving from her to the darkness that was quickly surrounding them.

"Can you pull it away?" he asked.

She shook her head no because the words failed her as two more ropes of darkness shot out from the shadows and wrapped themselves around Lawrence's ankles. Unlike hers, they pulled from within the opened door to the attic.

"Lawrence, no!" she said.

He slammed into the wooden floor hard, his head bouncing once and his rifle banging off the wooden boards with a thud. She tried to crawl to him, but the shadows began to pull her away. She could see his eyes, red with blood, struggled to stay open. Blood pooled beneath his chin and dripped from his lower lip.

"Get up!" she screamed.

She watched as his fingers squeezed themselves around the weapon. His knuckles whitened as he strengthened his grip and pushed with his elbows to lift himself from the ground. Burning lanced down her legs as she tried to crawl to him. He was almost back on his knees, the weapon cradled in his chest and one arm straight as it pressed him off the floor.

"I won't fail again," he whispered.

With a shaking hand, she tried to reach for his dusty coat. He was only inches away, but the darkness held her back.

"No!"

With another yank, Lawrence crashed to the floor when his body was pulled straight. His legs extended over the opening and the ladder, his eyes wide with anger and regret. She couldn't breathe, her throat tight as his gaze found hers.

"Forgive," he said before the darkness pulled and he fell down the ladder, the door to the attic slamming shut behind him.

He was gone, and she could no longer see. The tiny hands, little knives of evil, scratched at her skin as she pulled her knees up to her chest. It was over, it was all over.

Chapter 35

It felt like an hour had passed, maybe even a day, or only a few minutes. She could not tell. Lawrence, her neighbor, had been there to save her and now he was gone. Alone, she wanted to give in. Let the beast take her, end her misery and get her out of this darkness.

The attic no longer existed around her. She could feel the cold waves of darkness as it washed over her like pillowy clouds. Evil and sickness ran down her spine. She tried to cry, but nothing would come out. She was hollow, her insides red and raw. At first, she reasoned that if she got out of this alive, she would never be the same, she would be stronger, but that would never be the case. You didn't return from this. Children didn't survive this. These monsters never let anyone go. That is why parents called them make believe, warnings and fairytales that were used to teach them right from wrong.

There was nothing right with any of this. Her whole family was dead. She could feel it. She tried to imagine them in her mind, see their smiling faces, but they had already started to fade. Ghosts, in her mind and in reality. Whole to her, but without substance and without any real grounding in this world. Her world lost in a hell of darkness and despair.

BOOM!

Light exploded into the void, and her world spun within her head. Her stomach curled as it cramped within her and she fought the overwhelming urge to vomit. Pain wracked her shoulders and head, the dusty floor a hard recipient as she fell to it as if she had been suspended above the ground.

Boom!

A second hole, as large as her head, erupted in the door to the attic. She could see it again, and the darkness flooded toward the openings. With a thrust, the wooden barrier swung open with a crack as it split in half on the other side.

Like attack dogs, the evil rolled into the opening, baring its teeth at the intruders climbing the ladder to her dungeon.

"Liz!" her father yelled out.

Orange and yellow flames sparked as the darkness receded. Carrying a log with a rag wrapped around the top, her father's head popped out of the opening. Liz pushed herself off the floor as his homemade torch lead the way.

"Daddy!" she said, her voice a hoarse whisper.

"I'm here, baby. Don't you worry."

He was bloody. She could see the darkened streaks running down his neck and between the tendons that stretched his skin as he turned his head to search the room. His clothes were dark and black. Her breath caught in her throat at the sight of him. He was a walking pool of death. How he still stood, she did not know. Her hands quaked as he pulled himself fully into the room. She could see cuts all along his body through the material that stuck to his skin. He stank of death and bloody iron, but at the moment it was the sweetest thing she had ever smelt.

"Come here, Liz. We need to hurry."

He extended his open hand to her, and she felt his strong grip wrap itself around her wrist. With little effort, he pulled until she was on her feet. The blood was fresh on his hands, and standing close she could see his skin was pale where it wasn't stained red.

"He won't let me go, Daddy," she said with her face buried into his chest. "He won't let any of us go."

His arms pulled her close, and she could feel his strength run through her body. Her father would never let anything hurt her. She squeezed her arms as tight as she could, holding onto him so that the demon could not pull her back.

"Let him try," her father said with a tone that sent a wash of dread through her body.

Darkness materialized between them and their exit. Horns scratched the roof above, the fiery eyes of hell looking down at them from the rafters. Shoulders rippled with muscle and arms scarred with lines that crisscrossed over blackened skin extended from the shadows as claws of black ice reflected the burning fire of her father's torch.

"The child is mine. Punishment for sins of the father and the mother," the demon said. "You have been a very, very bad man, Robert."

It smiled, and she could see its black tongue. Its hooked nose and pointed goatee glared at her father as he stood between her and it, its power circling around them and choking out the light that protected them.

"You cannot have her. She will not pay for mistakes I have made."

The demon smiled, a hiss like a snake scratching at Liz's ears. "No one is immune to my punishment. You hold no power here."

Liz backed away when her father's hand, reached behind him and pressed against her chest. She could barely turn her eyes away. Now standing over eight feet tall, the monster took up the entire room from wall to wall. Her father was running his hand across his back. There was something tucked into the back of his shirt. A silver can.

"We'll have to see about that," he said as his fingers wrapped around the canister and then swung it around in front of him.

Fire burst out like the breath of a dragon as the spray hit the torch and ignited. Fire engulfed the monster from head to toe, the flames licking at the roof above and catching on the insulation like dried leaves. Heat and smoke began to fill the room, and Liz coughed as her lungs struggled for air.

"Fire? I was born in the fire!" the demon's voice thundered.

It stepped toward them, the flames flicking out as if its skin absorbed it like water. Her father didn't hesitate. A knife materialized in his hand, and he ran it through the creature's chest. Tearing hard, the thin blade exited the side with a spray of black bile, and the monster roared like a lion. Her father continued his attack after he ducked under a swipe from the demon's talons. A silver tip exited the darkened flesh between elbow and shoulder, separating the muscle as it sliced.

Liz could feel the droplets splattering across her face. Cold as ice, she wiped them away, her skin staining black as the devil turned and lunged at her father again. Injured or not, her dad danced around the creature and opened more wounds as black, darkened blood stained the walls and the floor at their feet. It rained gore as the room filled with smoke, thick and choking in thick clouds that rolled across the ceiling.

"Dad!" she screamed.

Her lungs burned to get that single word out. The light in her father's hand was fading, but not from the demon's magic. Liz could feel the sweat running down her face and neck as her skin sizzled beneath the heat. He did not react to her pleas for help. She began to crawl toward the opening, avoiding the flames to her left and the feet of both man and demon as their dance of death spun through the room.

"Dad!" she screamed over the roar of the flames and the thunderous howls of the monster.

All around them was lit up with fire. She reached out and pulled her head through the attic opening. Cool air pulled itself into the room, and she tried to fill her lungs, but they choked and forced her to cough instead. The ladder was within her reach. She took a deep breath, the oxygen cool and sweet in her chest as she wrapped her fingers around the first wooden rung. Almost there, only one more foot.

Her grip failed as her father crashed down next to her. The ground shifted as her body slipped and slid through the opening. Weightless, she watched as the dark opening to the room above the hallway receeded, and she fell. White light, bright and blinding, flashed before her eyes as an explosion erupted in her mind.

"I've got ya," a voice said as her body jerked to a stop.

She didn't hit the floor, though her skull pounded where it knotted at the center of her scalp. It was Lawrence. Blood soaked his face, but his eyes looked at her, wide and awake. They were as red as he was, with a tint of yellow that reminded her of a cat.

"We've got to go, now!" he said. "Can you walk?"

Her eyes turned to the doorway above.

"Dad!"

Thunder shook the ceiling above them and cracks rippled the wall. Light danced with the shadows above as the fire began to consume the attic floor and bubbled the boards above their heads.

A shadow jumped over the opening, appearing before the light and disappearing just as quick.

"Your dad can take care of himself," Lawrence said.

He put her down on her feet and pushed her toward her parents' bedroom door. For the first time, she could hear Stevie crying. His wails of terror vibrated her eardrums. He had to be hysterical. She had never heard fear like this coming from a baby. Stepping around her, Lawrence raced for the bedroom door. Throwing it open, the gray light that had shown her the monster's power rolled out of the room. Her brother was standing in his crib. Cheeks puffy with tears, he reached out to the man who had run in to save him. Regardless of the gore that clung to him, her baby brother wrapped his arms and chubby fingers around his neck. She could see his chest heaving as he cried.

"Hurry, now run!" he ordered.

Wood paneling splintered and fell from above their heads and crashed to the floor at the far end of the hallway. Liz took another look at the stairs. Where was her father? Another roar shook the building at her feet, and a shadow slid down the stairs. With a thud, the body slipped and rolled itself to the railing that stopped it from falling to the foyer below.

"Dad!"

She ran to him, pushing away Lawrence's hand as he tried to steer her to the stairs.

"I'm all right. Get out of here, now," he said through coughs that shook his chest.

Wrapping her hands under his arms, she tried to pull him to his feet. He weighed more than the world itself, and her hands felt tiny against the muscles that flexed on his back. Using her as a small balance, she pressed herself against him as he rolled and stood on his feet.

"Come on!" Lawrence yelled out before he took the first step down the stairs.

Hands pressed against her back, her father kept her in front of him as his feet stayed only a few inches behind her heels and his body curled over her shoulders. She could feel his hot breath warming the back of her head, his presence forcing her to move faster.

They covered the stairs two at a time, Lawrence and her baby brother in the lead, and her father and herself only a step behind.

"What about Mom?" Liz asked when they reached the last step and Lawrence made no hesitation for the front door that hung open with a hole the size of her head where the doorknob once was.

Her father tightened a grip on her shoulder, his fingers pressing until pain ran down her collarbone.

"Your mother is gone. We can't stay here any longer," he said.

She knew why, but the words still hurt. A feeling of loss appeared in her chest, but she swallowed hard to force it away. Her mother had made her choice, kissing that man Tony and watching as they hurt her father. Maybe it was best she didn't know what had happened to her.

"Robert!" her mother's voice screamed out.

All four of them skidded to a halt a few feet from their exit. Turning, they all could see her mother silhouetted in the doorway. Wild-eyed and disheveled, Liz had never seen her like this. She was always in control and always presentable. Yet now her hair was crinkled and stuck on end around her head like she had been electrocuted in an old movie. Blood and dirt running down her pale skin, her ruby red lips darkened against the white of her teeth as she bared them like a wild dog.

"Look what you did to me. You and that little monster. Leave me my baby and go!" she said.

There was a knife in her hand, and she raised it above her head. Liz stepped back as her father positioned himself between them.

"It's over, Amy. I know what you did, and the Detective probably does as well. We don't have time for this, you saw what lives in this house," her father answered.

What Detective? Liz didn't have time to ask, but she could see the flames growing, and the heat was reaching her skin down where she stood at the door. The whole house would soon be on fire, and she could see the black magic building behind the woman she called her mother. Anger did not allow her mom to see it. The knife's tip wavered as it reflected the light above her head, her eyes darting between Stevie in her neighbor's hand and her father.

"Let's all get out of here. I'm taking the children, but you still have time to get out," her father said.

He took a step back, and Liz followed so that he wouldn't step on her. Lawrence turned to the door, Stevie screaming on his shoulder as Liz watched the black clouds rise up behind her mom. She never noticed as they filled the room behind her, her stance widened and blood dripping from where her teeth bit down on her lower lip.

"Last chance, Robert!" she screamed.

Liz gasped and squeezed against her father's back as the demon's black talons erupted through her mom's blouse. Once white, they were now dripping black and red as her blood drained out in a flood. Her mother barely made a sound as the monster tore its hand back out and her body dropped with a crash. It stood looking at them from across the room.

"You will not leave this house," its voice thundered from all around them.

Liz took another step back with her father, the wounds on the devil all healed as its eyes glared with the fire that burned within it. Taking another step back, Liz stumbled as her ankle rolled against Lawrence's shoe. Squeezing onto her father's shirt, she spun to see that the man had fallen to his knees, Stevie still cradled in his arms. His eyes stared off to the darkened corner, opposite where the demon prepared to play its final game.

"Take your brother, sweetie," Lawrence said through gritted teeth.

She reached around him and picked Stevie out of his embrace. His hands were shaking, and sweat ran down his wrinkled forehead. His eyes did not leave the empty corner.

"Detective, come on!" her father shouted.

Liz looked back, her brother balanced on her hip and burying himself into her neck. She could feel his warmth against her skin as her blood felt ice cold. The monster was advancing. It smiled as its horns scratched at the ceiling of the foyer, and black smoke rolled in its wake.

"Leave me!" her fallen neighbor shouted as he waived her father forward.

Gripping her shirt sleeve, her father pulled her through the door. The monster, the devil that wanted all their lives, did not give chase. Liz stayed in her father's footsteps as they raced down the steps and up the path toward the cars. Lights and sirens lit up between the branches of the trees that led to their house. Fire trucks and police cars spilled into their front yard.

Turning back, Liz pulled away from her father's grip as she took a final look back at her house. Lawrence, her neighbor, the man who came out of nowhere to try and save them, stood in the doorway. The light of the fire that held the darkness at bay silhouetted his body as he stood with his shoulders wide and a pistol held in his left hand. She could see the fire red eyes bearing down on him, but he did not falter. He was not alone as he stood defiantly in the doorway. A little girl, barely up to his chest, stood with him. She was gray, and the shadows shied away from her as if she had a light of her own. Liz shrugged her father's arms away again, taking a step closer as she struggled to see more. A teddy bear dangled in the girl's arm as she stood at Lawrence's side. They both stared back at the demon who roared, and Liz could feel the vibrations at her feet, the frozen ground rumbling with the power. A tiny hand, without color, reached up and slipped its fingers in between Lawrence's bloody grip. Liz gasped as the girl's skin brightened and filled with life. Long brown hair waved its way down to the middle of her back, and her clothes brightened with the radiance of a child's pink and baby blue pajamas. Thunder bellowed from the demon once again as the house's front door slammed shut, the crack so loud that Liz took a step back and huddled herself against her father.

Chapter 36

Her front yard looked like the end of some action movie or other show that her father enjoyed on television. Except this time, it was as real as the cold that bit against her skin regardless of the thick wool blanket she pulled tightly against her body. Lights flashed against a backdrop of dark green trees and white snow, as though they belonged to monsters dozens of feet high stomping through the forest alcove with silent steps hidden below the rumble of engines and pumps.

Her house continued to burn as she sat on the back of the ambulance, her cheek stinging from the bandages they taped to her face. She could feel her skin swelling, and her cheekbone throbbed every time she moved her jaw. The skin of her legs still burned from where the demon had wrapped itself around her.

There would be very little scars on her body when this was all over, but the worst of what would remain would be inside. She watched as the orange flames reached high into the air, dark smoke rolling into the colorless sky above. The firetrucks had tried to save her home, bringing two tanks with hoses, but the water was useless against the flames that consumed it all. The more they tried, the hotter the house burned. She could tell they only went through the motions now and made sure the disaster didn't spread to the forest around them. They moved slowly and some joked with words she couldn't hear, but the laughter and ease at which they went about their duties told her everything.

This wasn't their home, it was hers, and it was all lost. She pulled the blanket tighter against her shoulders, fingers of ice sneaking in as a soft breeze carried with it the acrid smell of burning wood and gasoline from the dozen emergency vehicles that spread themselves through the snow.

"Everything is going to be fine, beautiful," the EMT said.

She smiled back at him. He was young, like those men who had done this to her were, with shaved brown hair and soft eyes that narrowed when he smiled at her. He was trying his best, but he hadn't survived what she saw. Did she actually survive? Was she still herself after all that? She didn't know. Inside was raw and swollen. So beaten, she felt numb to everything and everyone, their words and their emotions so far away she could only think about what it felt like to smile and laugh.

It was now after midnight, Christmas morning, and her home was a pile of burning rubble and ash. Her mother was dead with her murderous boyfriend, and her father was strapped to a bed in the ambulance next to her.

"Can I go see my dad?" she asked.

The young EMT looked over to the other vehicle, its rear door still open and Stevie bouncing on the female medic's shoulder.

"I don't think that would be a problem. You come right back though if anything else hurts."

She nodded to him and pushed away from the ambulance. Her legs ached as she walked toward the others, her entire body tired from her ordeal she knew she'd never get over.

"Dad, how do you feel?" she whispered when she reached his side.

His skin was pale, pulled tight against the angular bones of his face, but they had cleaned most of the gore from his body. He was strapped down by brown leather collars that prevented him from moving his left arm and both of his legs. His shirt was cut away, the bloody cloth discarded to the floor. White gauze and tape covered most of his stomach and ribs, stretched to try and hold everything that made him who he was inside. She could see his chest rising slowly before his own blanket was draped over him.

"I feel like I've been hit by a truck, but I've seen worse," he answered.

He tried to smile and lift his head, but a second female EMT was quick to press down on his shoulder and keep him steady.

"Don't move. We've stopped your bleeding for now, but we still need to get you to a hospital," the woman said.

She was older than he was, with wrinkles that reached far and wide from the corner of her eyes, but Liz could see the laugh lines that extended from her soft lips. None of those that surrounded her looked upset to be out here, medics and police standing around her home on a night they should be with their families. This was a nice community; too bad she'd only been here a week, and they'd soon have to leave again. They always did.

"Mr. Robert O'Maille, I'd like to have a word with you," an officer said.

Liz jumped out of the way as the large man materialized from around the corner of the emergency vehicle. He towered over the EMTs, and his head was only a few inches short of the roof that opened to the back of the truck. The man's shadow extended far from the heels of his boots, the bright light inside the ambulance making him appear ten times larger than he was as his uniform and badge shone brightly like stars pinned to his chest.

"Mr. O'Maille isn't in any condition to answer questions, officer," the EMT sitting next to her dad said.

"Captain, and it will only take a second," he said before his eyes turned back to where her father lay with his dark eyes locked on the policeman. Liz could see the tight lips and firm jaw that said that no matter what the ladies did, he was going to get his words in now. "Detective Marc Stutton had taken an interest in you. I got the call that he was coming here tonight. You wouldn't happen to know about his whereabouts, now would you?"

Her father rolled his eyes. Detective Marc Stutton? Did he mean Lawrence? Thinking about it, she was almost certain her dad had called him Detective, but the night was already fading into a haze, memories she knew would only return in the darkest of nightmares. Her father tried to lift his hand, but it was quickly slapped back down.

"Yeah, he was here," her father answered, the finger of his right hand pointing toward their house that was now no more than a lower floor with its roof caved in.

"I see. We'll talk again at the hospital, Mr. O'Maille."

The officer nodded to both EMTs and Stevie before turning back to the row of cars with their lights flashing blue, red and white.

"He helped save our lives," Liz said.

The captain stopped in his tracks, his head half-cocked to the right as his eyes met hers.

"He rushed in when my mom and those men tried to hurt my father. If it weren't for him we would have never gotten out," Liz said. She pulled the blanket tight enough she worried it would rip and fall to the ground, but thinking of the demon inside that house made sure it never felt tight enough. "He stayed behind to fight the demon when my father carried us out."

"I see," the captain nodded.

She didn't know if he believed her, and she didn't care. No one would. She was old enough to understand that. They would think she was just frightened, her mind lost to her imagination to escape the horror she saw at the hands of those inside her house. Her father would believe her, though; he would have the scars to prove it.

"Captain, now that you've had your chance to question an injured man and his frightened daughter, we have a few questions for you," a dark man asked.

The captain stopped before he could get two steps away from Liz when two men in long black coats exited a dark car that had sat silently next to the ambulances. Both men matched the captain in height and size as one approached from in front of him and the other positioned himself between the officer and her father.

"And who would you be?" The captain asked.

"Marshal White and Marshal Wallace. U.S. Marshal Service, and we would like to have a word with you about Mr. Smith and his family," the man who stood inches from the captain's face said.

"Who is Mr. Smith?" The captain asked before turning his gaze over his shoulder to Liz and her father.

"Exactly," the marshal said as he placed a large gloved hand onto the captain's back and began to lead him toward their car.

The closest marshal turned and nodded toward her father, who returned a thumbs up before his hand was slapped away again by the EMT. Liz looked up at the man. His dark skin and bald head melted into the sky above, but his eyes were bright and his smile warm.

"It will be OK, we'll take it from here," he said and then turned to follow as the captain was led away.

Liz turned to what remained of her family. She didn't know if it would be OK, but they were still alive. With a last look at the house, she took a deep breath and climbed up beside her father, placing her hand on his bandaged arm for comfort.

"Merry Christmas, Dad."

About the Author

Known for the darker themes of his writing, RJ currently sits with the published novel Dark Choices (Nov. 2015), Trail of Darkness (Dec. 2016) and the short stories Goodbye Daddy, Family Reunion, and Angel on the Edge.

The father of a four-year-old boy, RJ currently resides in central Pennsylvania where he works, plays, and dreams through the worlds he writes in. All of his works can be found anywhere you buy your favorite books.

@WorldsbyRoh

www.goodreads.com/RJ_Seymour

roh(At)worldsbyroh(dot)com

www.worldsbyroh.com

Other Book Furnace Titles

Goodbye Daddy (Short Story)
Family Reunion (Short Story)
Angel on the Edge (Short Story)
Dark Choices

CPSIA information can be obtained
at www.ICGtesting.com
Printed in the USA
BVOW08*1143020217
474973BV00017B/34/P

9 781943 266036